Dear parents, caregivers, and educators:

If you want to get your child excited about reading, you've come to the right place! Ready-to-Read *GRAPHICS* is the perfect launchpad for emerging graphic novel readers.

All Ready-to-Read *GRAPHICS* books include the following:

★ **A how-to guide to reading graphic novels for first-time readers**

★ **Easy-to-follow panels to support reading comprehension**

★ **Accessible vocabulary to build your child's reading confidence**

★ **Compelling stories that star your child's favorite characters**

★ **Fresh, engaging illustrations that provide context and promote visual literacy**

Wherever your child may be on their reading journey, Ready-to-Read *GRAPHICS* will make them giggle, gasp, and want to keep reading more.

Blast off on this starry adventure . . . a universe of graphic novel reading awaits!

ALL KETCHUP, NO MUSTARD!

written and illustrated by
JASON THARP

Ready-to-Read *GRAPHICS*

SIMON SPOTLIGHT

An imprint of Simon & Schuster Children's Publishing Division • New York • London • Toronto • Sydney • New Delhi
1230 Avenue of the Americas, New York, New York 10020 • This Simon Spotlight edition June 2021
Text and illustrations copyright © 2021 by Jason Tharp • All rights reserved, including the right of reproduction in whole or in part in any form.
SIMON SPOTLIGHT, READY-TO-READ, and colophon are registered trademarks of Simon & Schuster, Inc. For information about special discounts for bulk purchases,
please contact Simon & Schuster Special Sales at 1-866-506-1949 or business@simonandschuster.com. Manufactured in the United States of America 0521 LAK
1 2 3 4 5 6 7 8 9 10 • This book has been cataloged with the Library of Congress.
ISBN 978-1-5344-8463-4 (hc) • ISBN 978-1-5344-8462-7 (pbk) • ISBN 978-1-5344-8464-1 (ebook)

To all the BIG dreamers,

Be yourself, stay kind, and try every day.
The right people will find you!
And to Beth, Laura, Siobhan, and Nicole,
K.E.T.C.H.U.P. Crusaders indeed!

—J. T.

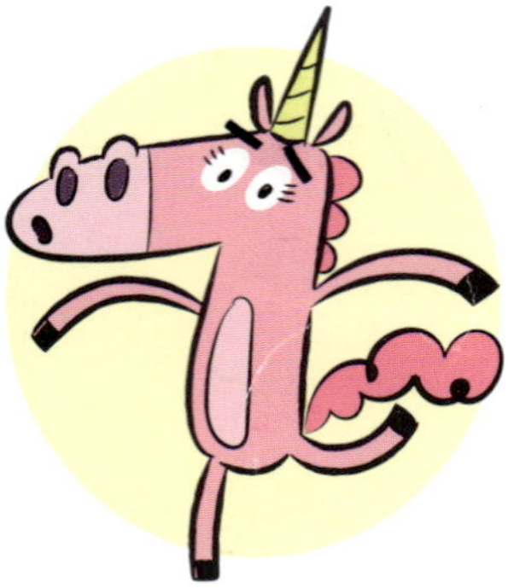

Aunt Corny

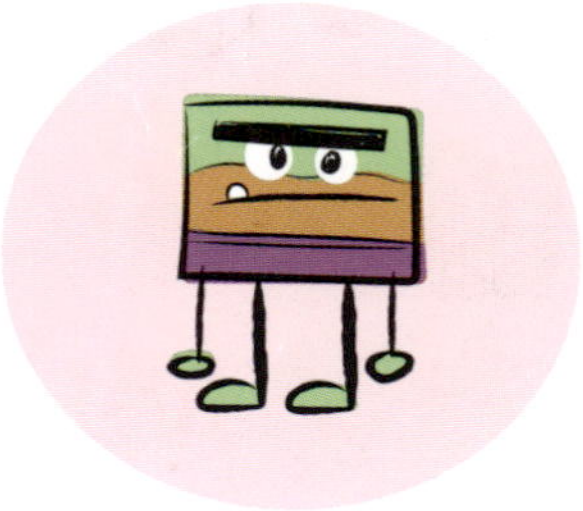

Crouton
(say: KROO-tahn)

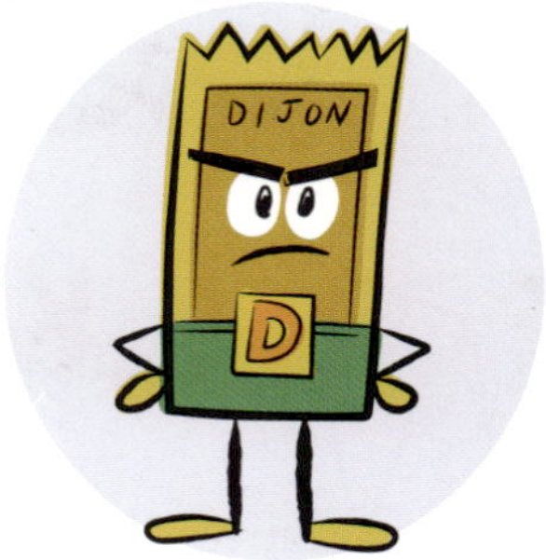
DIJON
D

Dijon (say: dee-ZHON)
Mustard

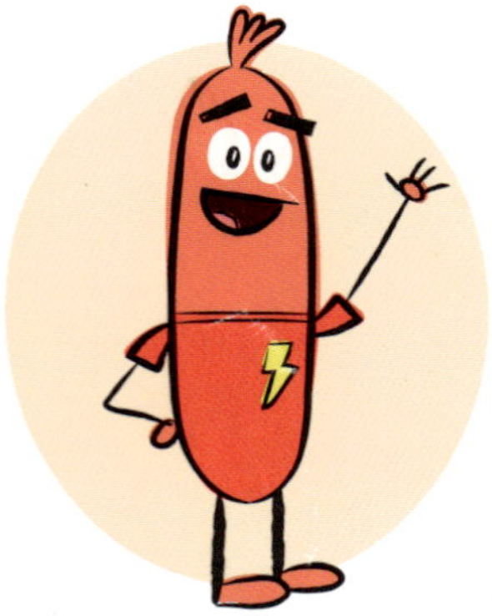

Dog

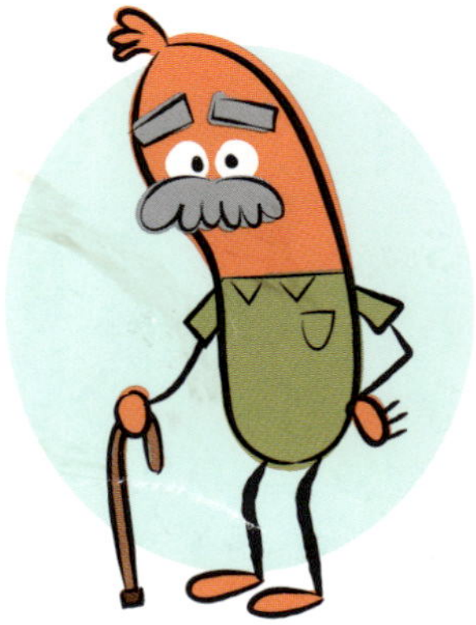

Great-Grandpa
Frank Furter

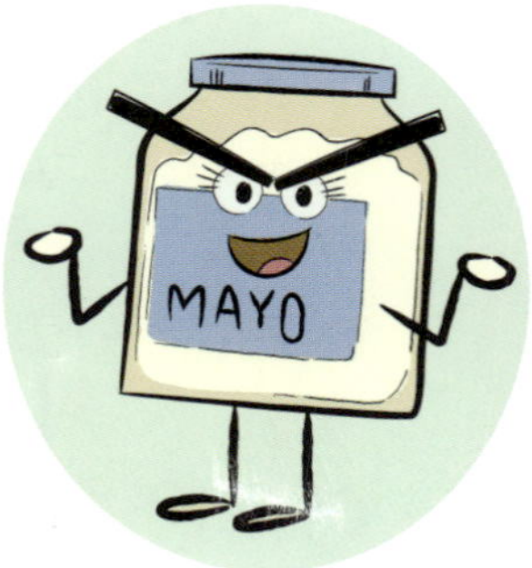
MAYO

Mayo Naze

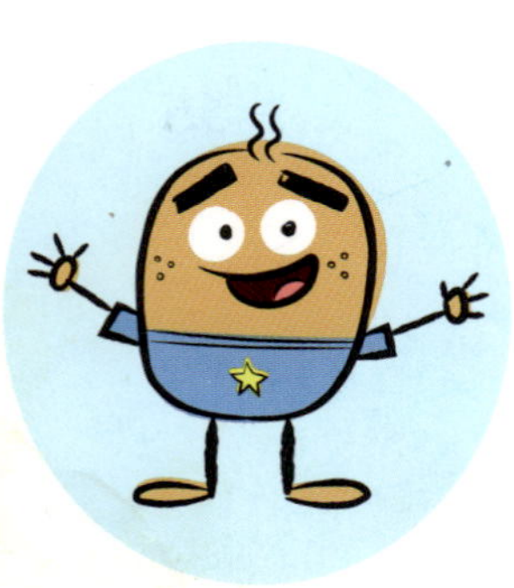

Nugget

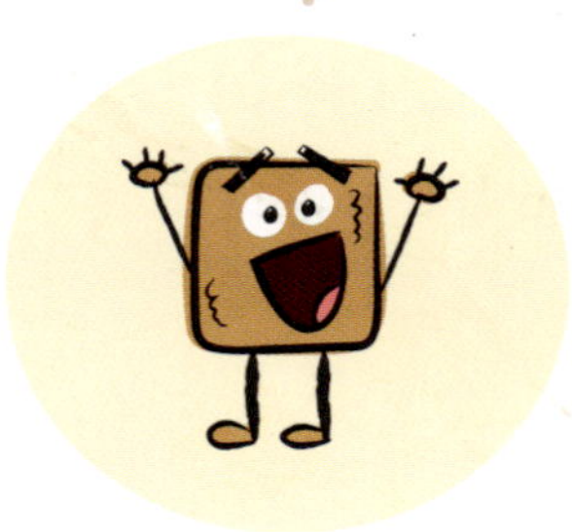

Tater Todd

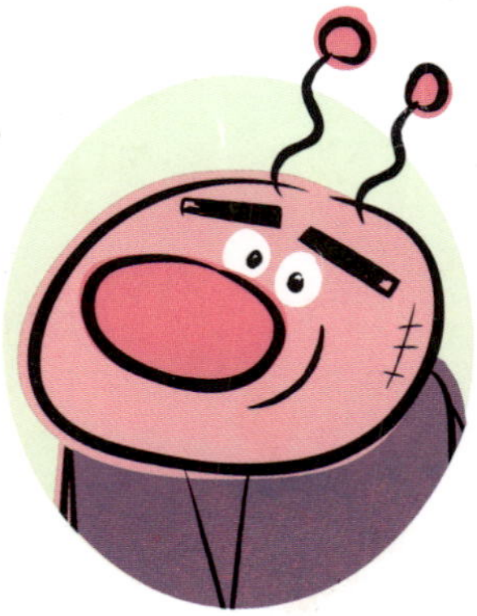

Stomp

CONTENTS

How to Read This Book

This is Dog. He is here to give you some tips on how to read this book.

If there is a box like this one, read the words inside the box first. Then read the words in the speech or thought bubbles below it...

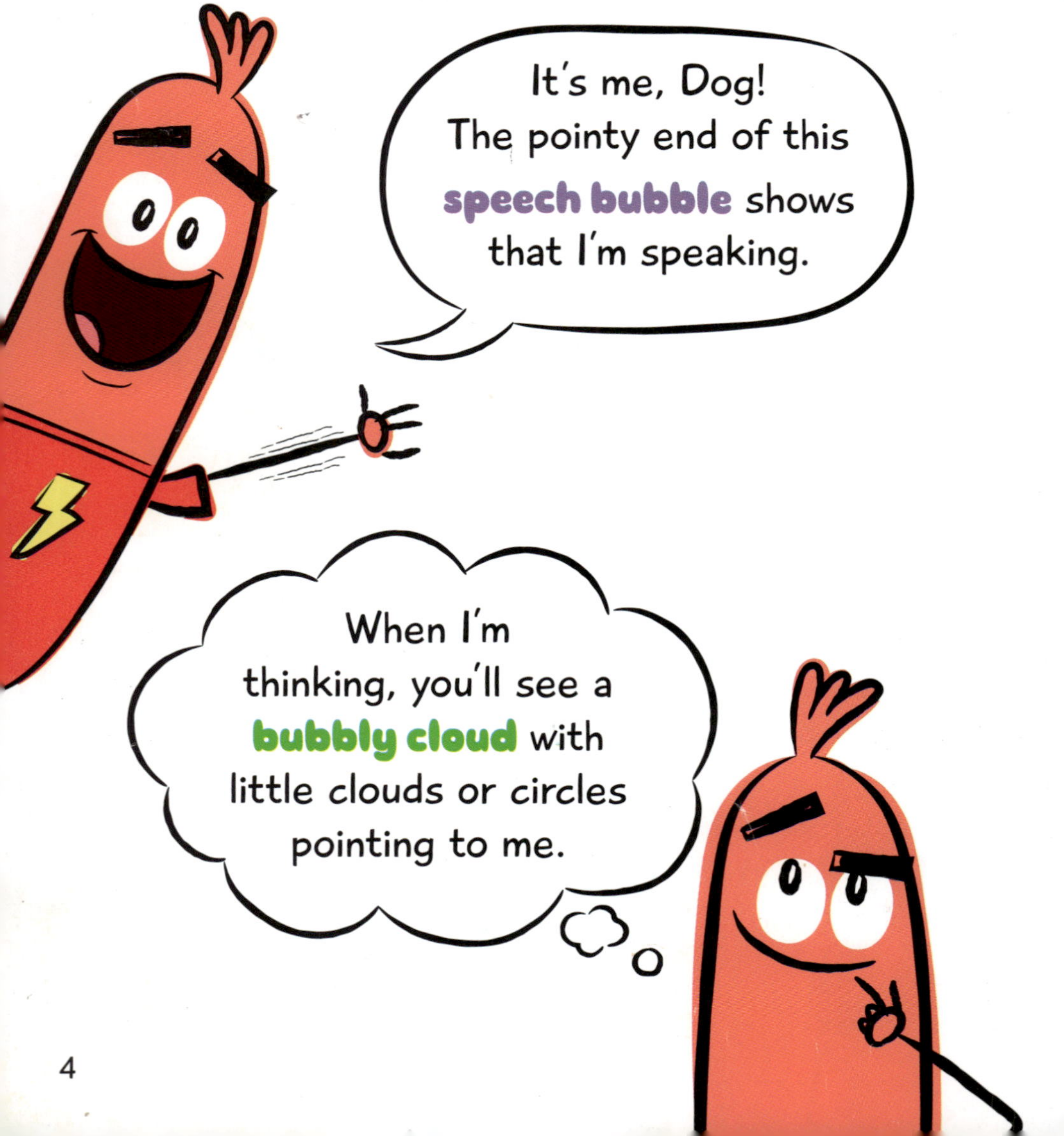
It's me, Dog! The pointy end of this speech bubble shows that I'm speaking.
When I'm thinking, you'll see a bubbly cloud with little clouds or circles pointing to me.

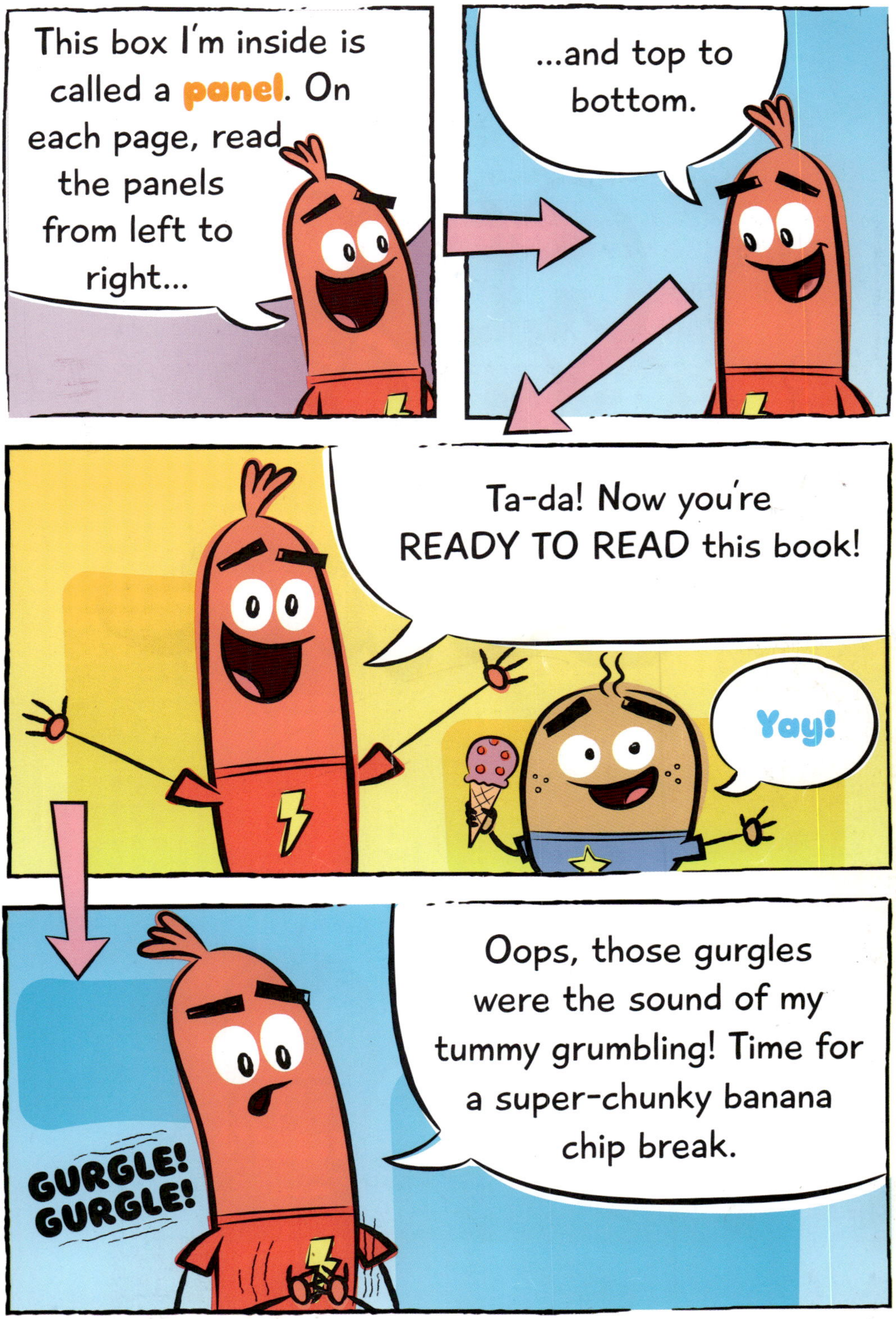
This box I'm inside is called a panel. On each page, read the panels from left to right...
...and top to bottom.
Ta-da! Now you're READY TO READ this book!
Yay!
GURGLE! GURGLE!
Oops, those gurgles were the sound of my tummy grumbling! Time for a super-chunky banana chip break.

Chapter 1

AND SO IT BEGINS

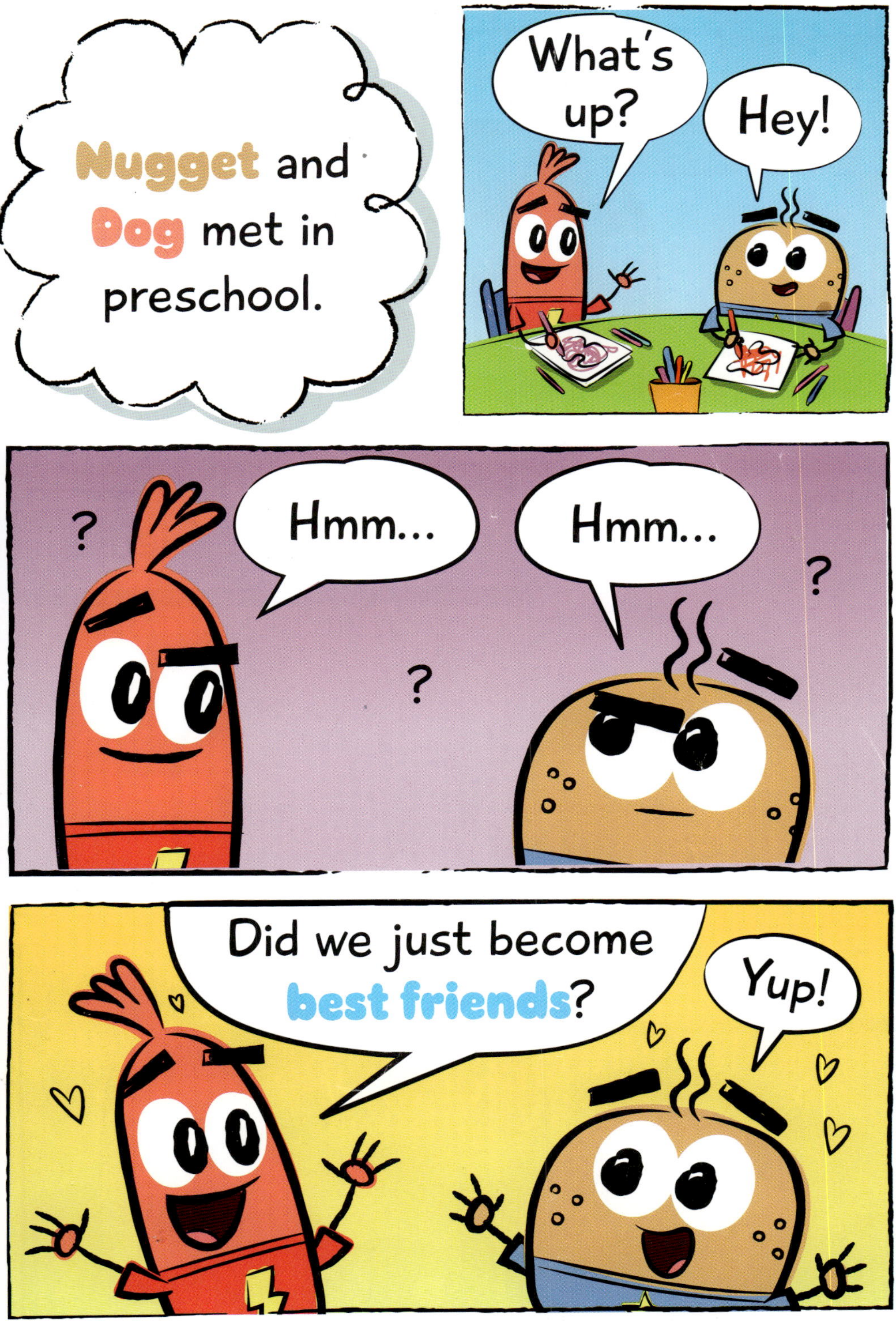
Nugget and Dog met in preschool.
What's up?
Hey!
Hmm...
Hmm...
?
?
?
Did we just become best friends?
Yup!

FAST FORWARD TO NOW...

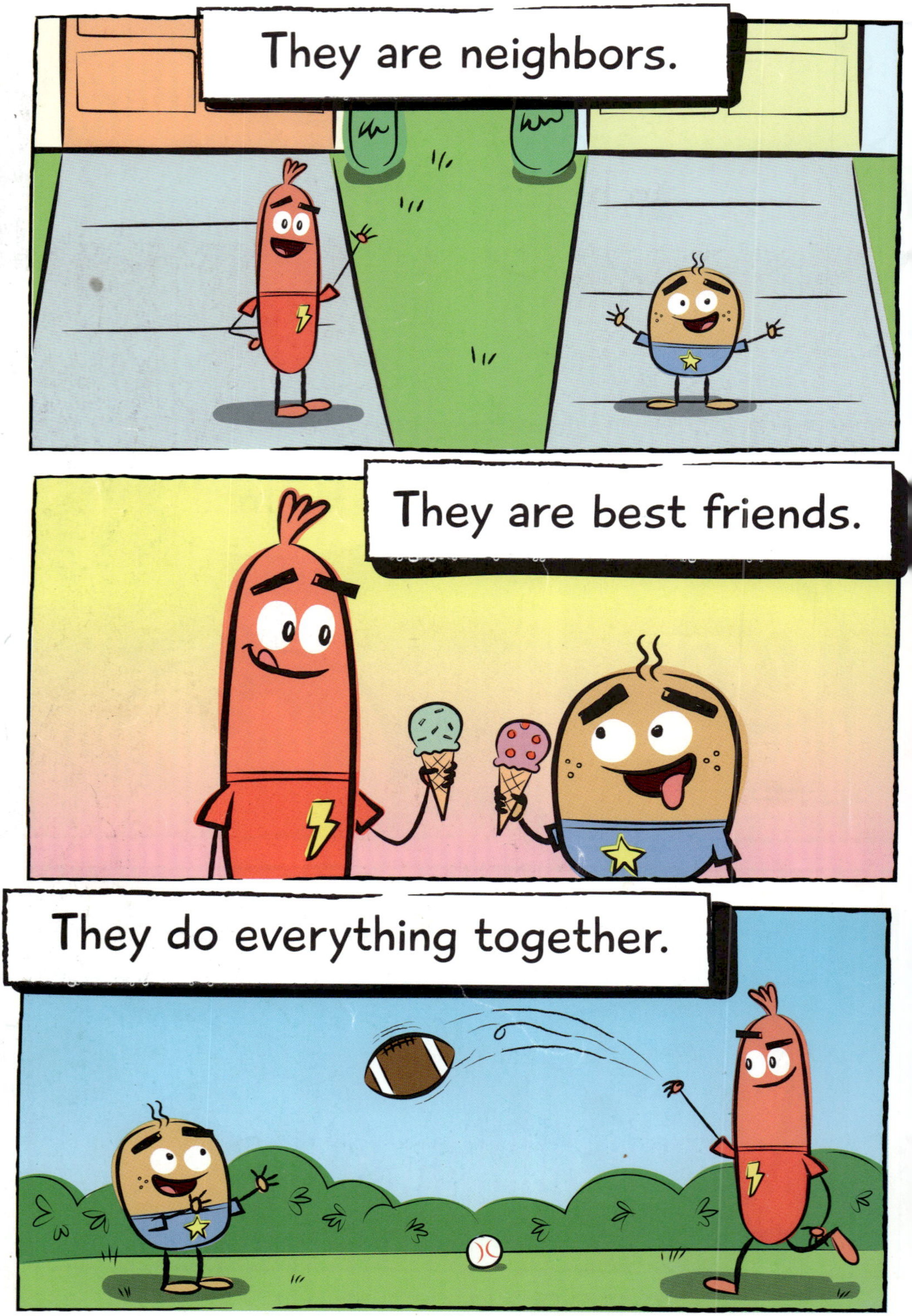
They are neighbors.
They are best friends.
They do everything together.

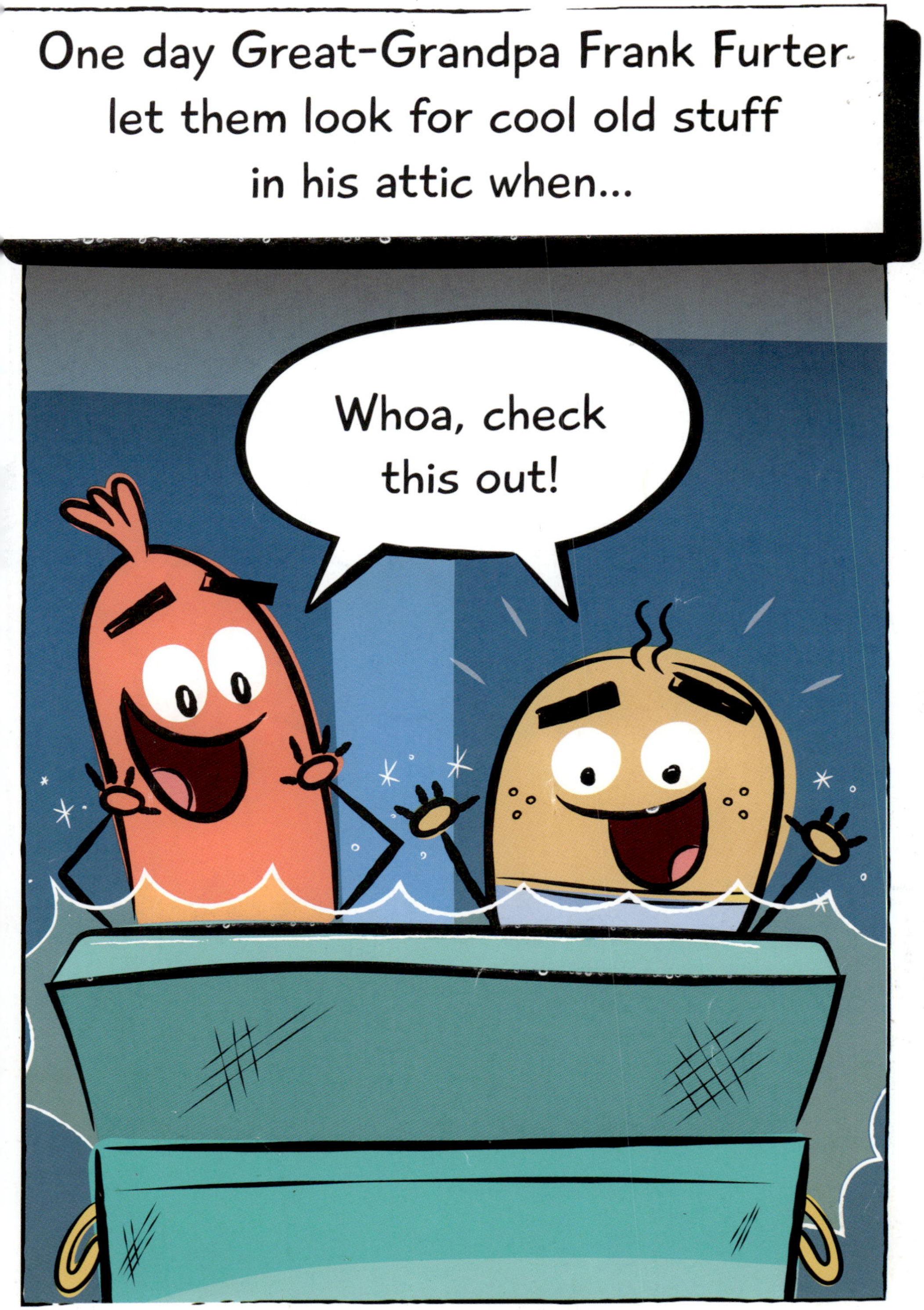
One day Great-Grandpa Frank Furter let them look for cool old stuff in his attic when...
Whoa, check this out!

Chapter 2

EVIL AND TANGY

DIJON

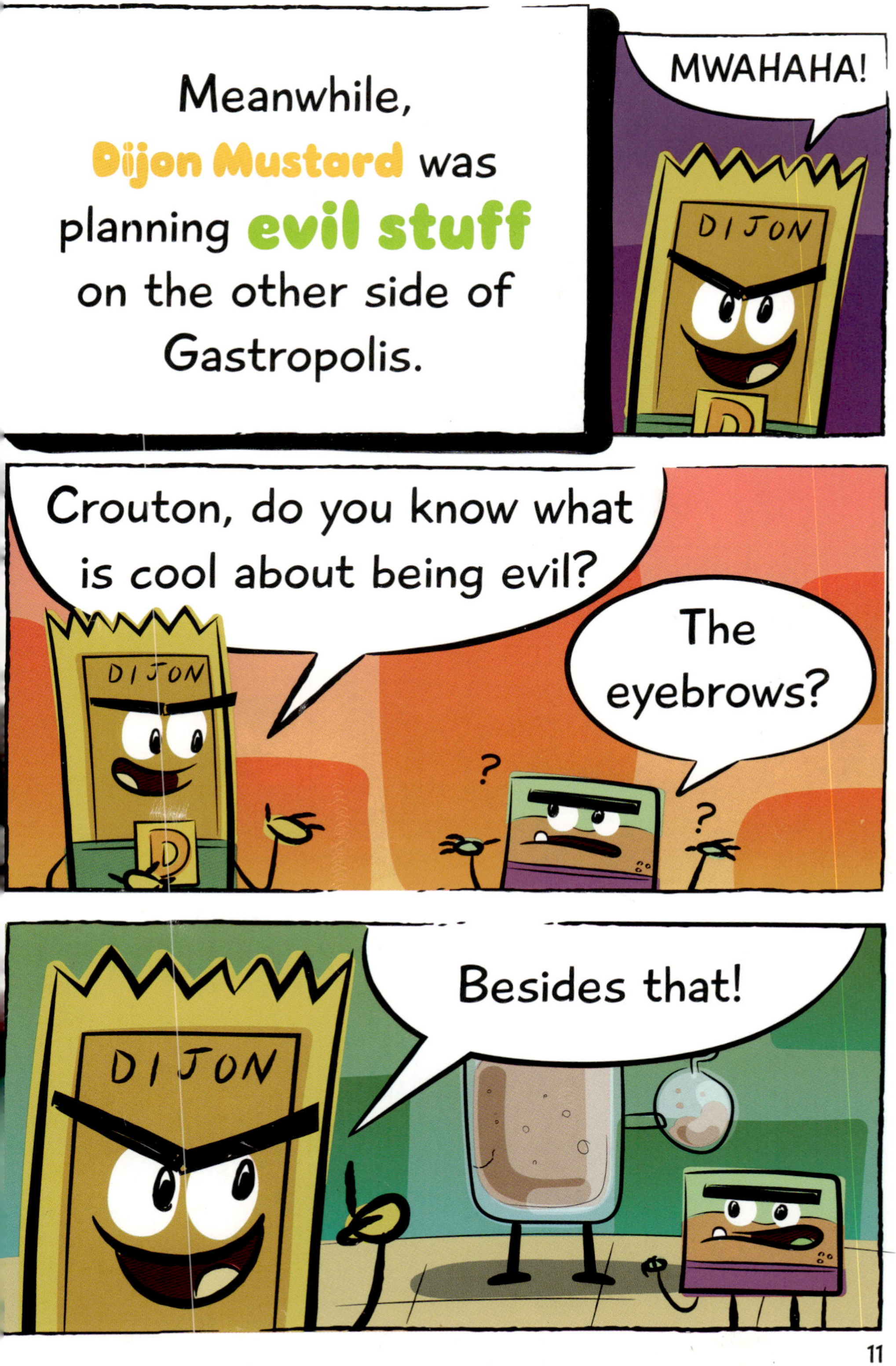
Meanwhile, Dijon Mustard was planning evil stuff on the other side of Gastropolis.
MWAHAHA!
DIJON
Crouton, do you know what is cool about being evil?
The eyebrows?
Besides that!

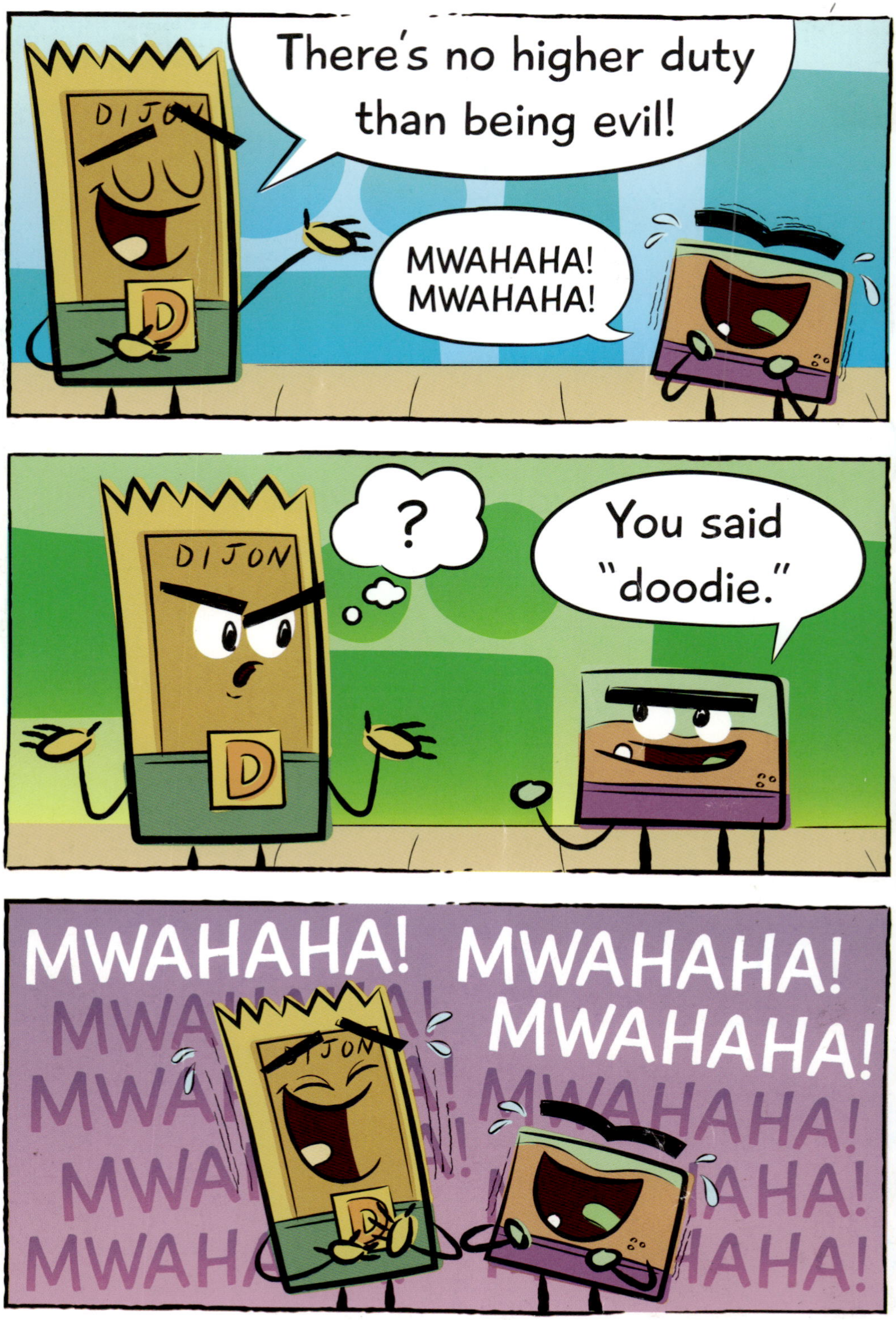
DIJON
There's no higher duty than being evil!
MWAHAHA! MWAHAHA!
DIJON
?
You said "doodie."
MWAHAHA! MWAHAHA! MWAHAHA!
DIJON

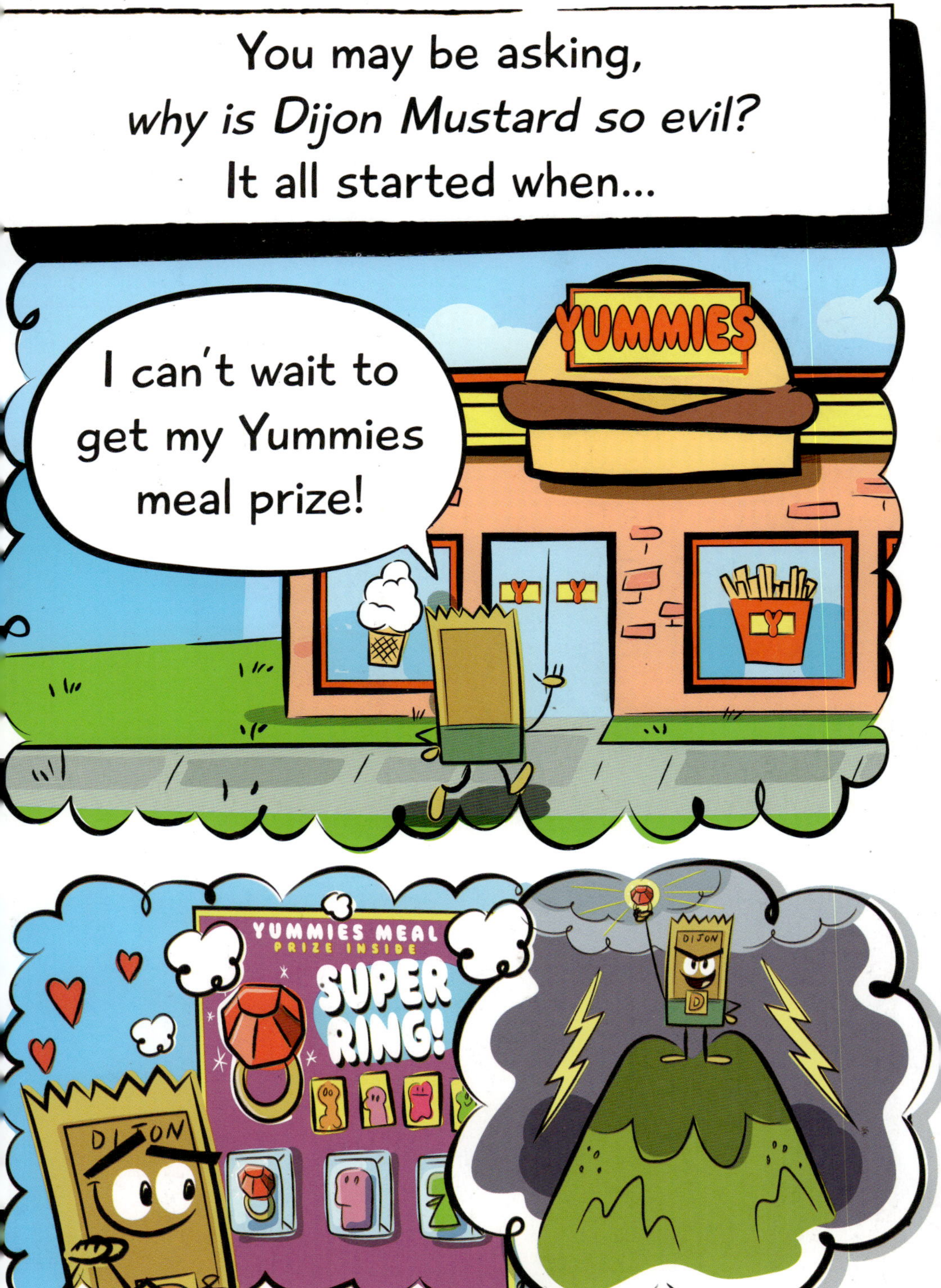
You may be asking,
why is Dijon Mustard so evil?
It all started when...
YUMMIES
I can't wait to get my Yummies meal prize!
YUMMIES MEAL
PRIZE INSIDE
SUPER RING!
DIJON
DIJON

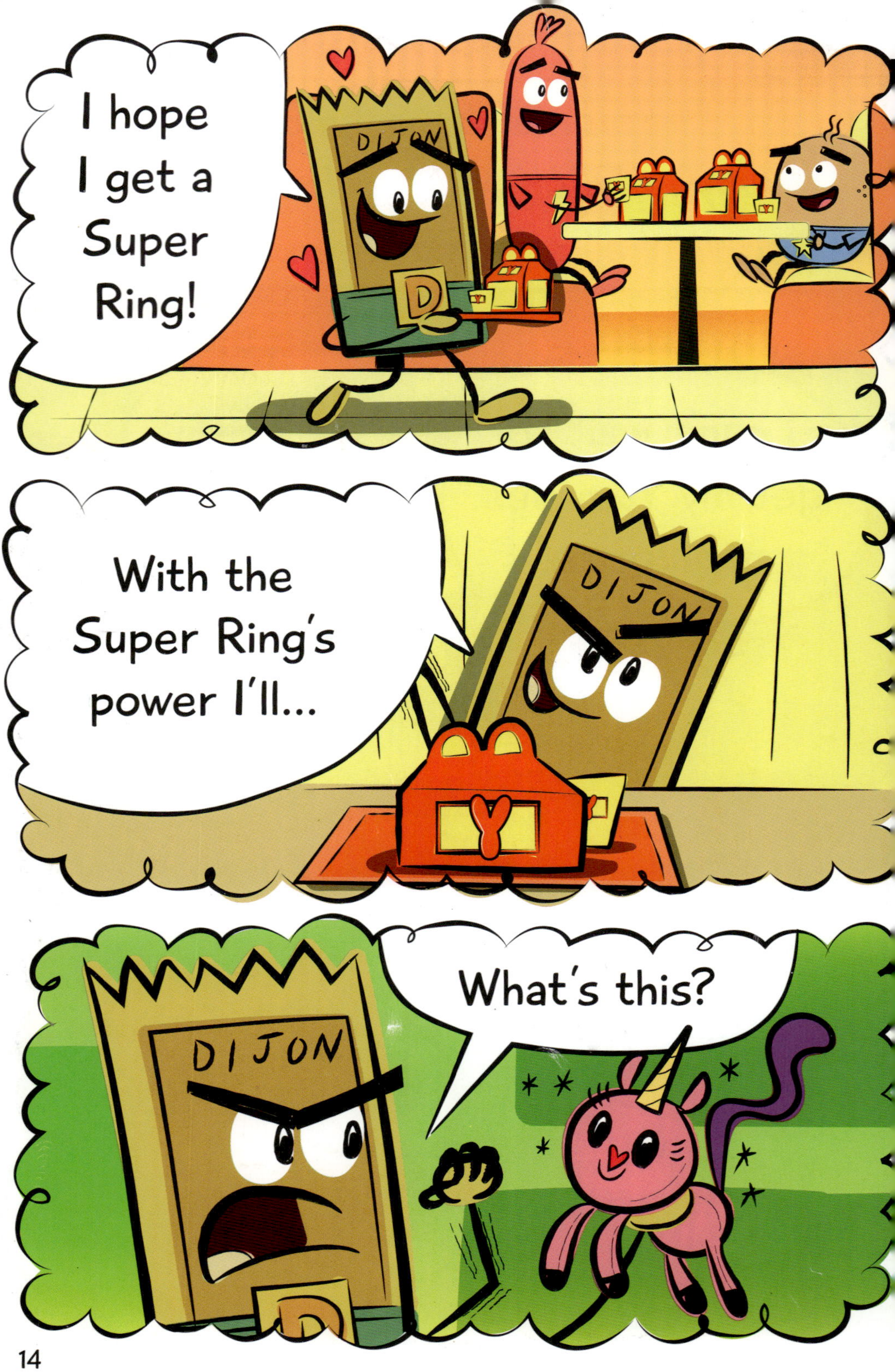
I hope I get a Super Ring!
DIJON
With the Super Ring's power I'll...
DIJON
What's this?
DIJON

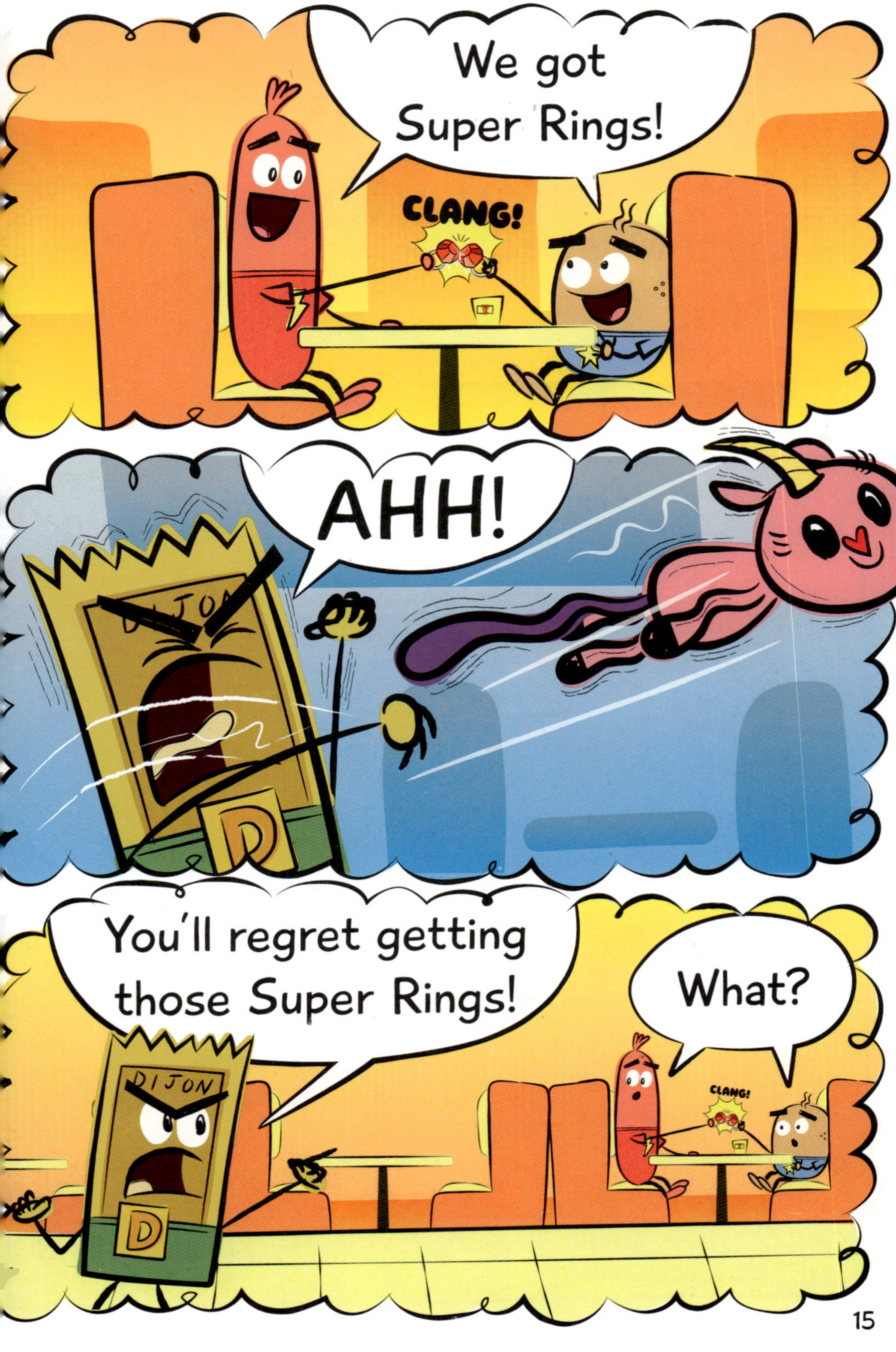
We got Super Rings!
CLANG!
AHH!
DIJON
D
You'll regret getting those Super Rings!
What?
CLANG!
DIJON
D

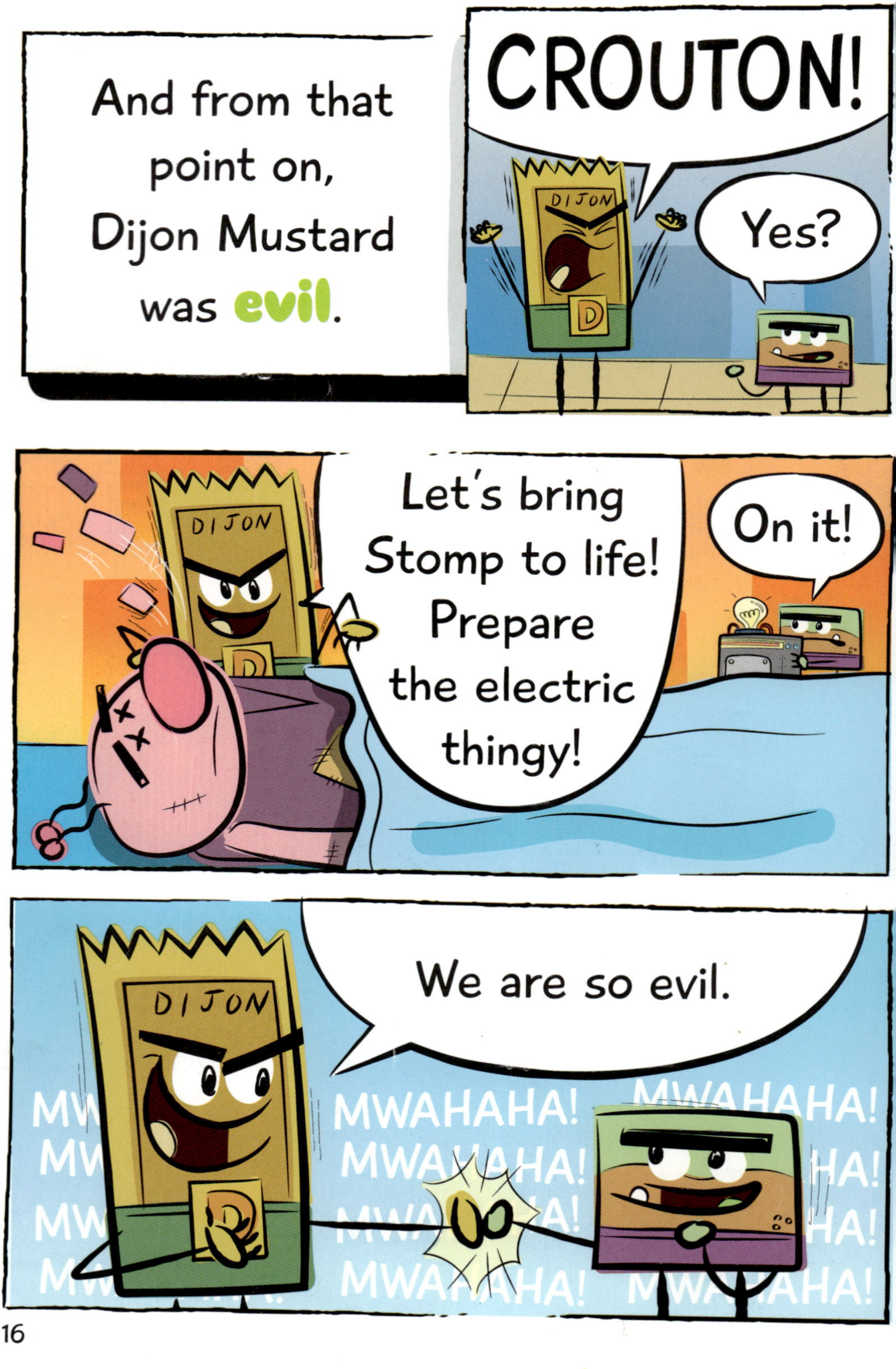
And from that point on, Dijon Mustard was evil.
CROUTON!
Yes?
DIJON
D
Let's bring Stomp to life! Prepare the electric thingy!
On it!
DIJON
D
We are so evil.
DIJON
D
MWAHAHA!
MWAHAHA!
MWAHAHA!
MWAHAHA!

Chapter 3

K.E.T.C.H.U.P.

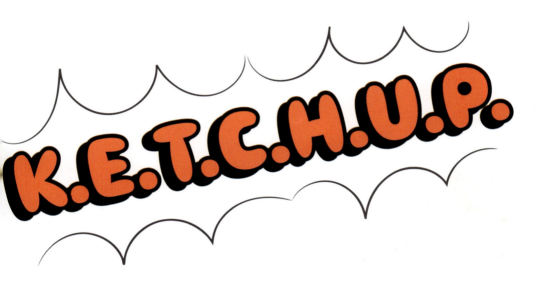

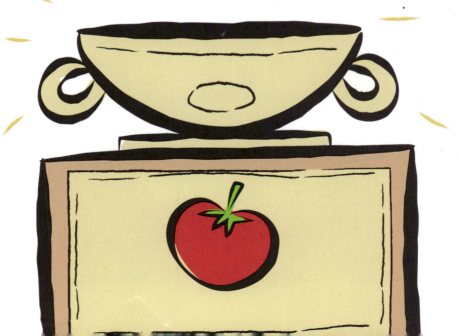

Meanwhile, Nugget and Dog were opening the cool box.

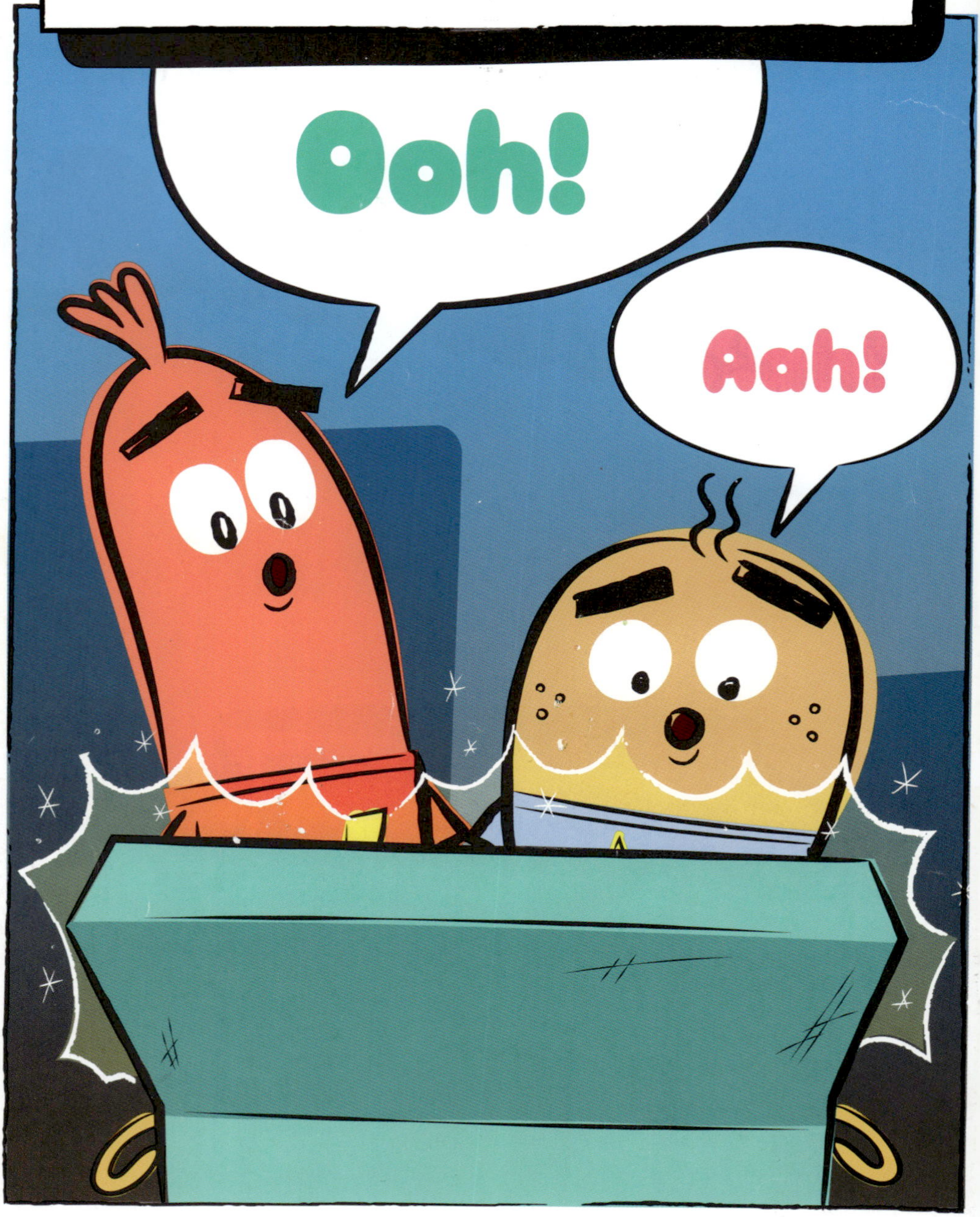
Ooh!
Aah!

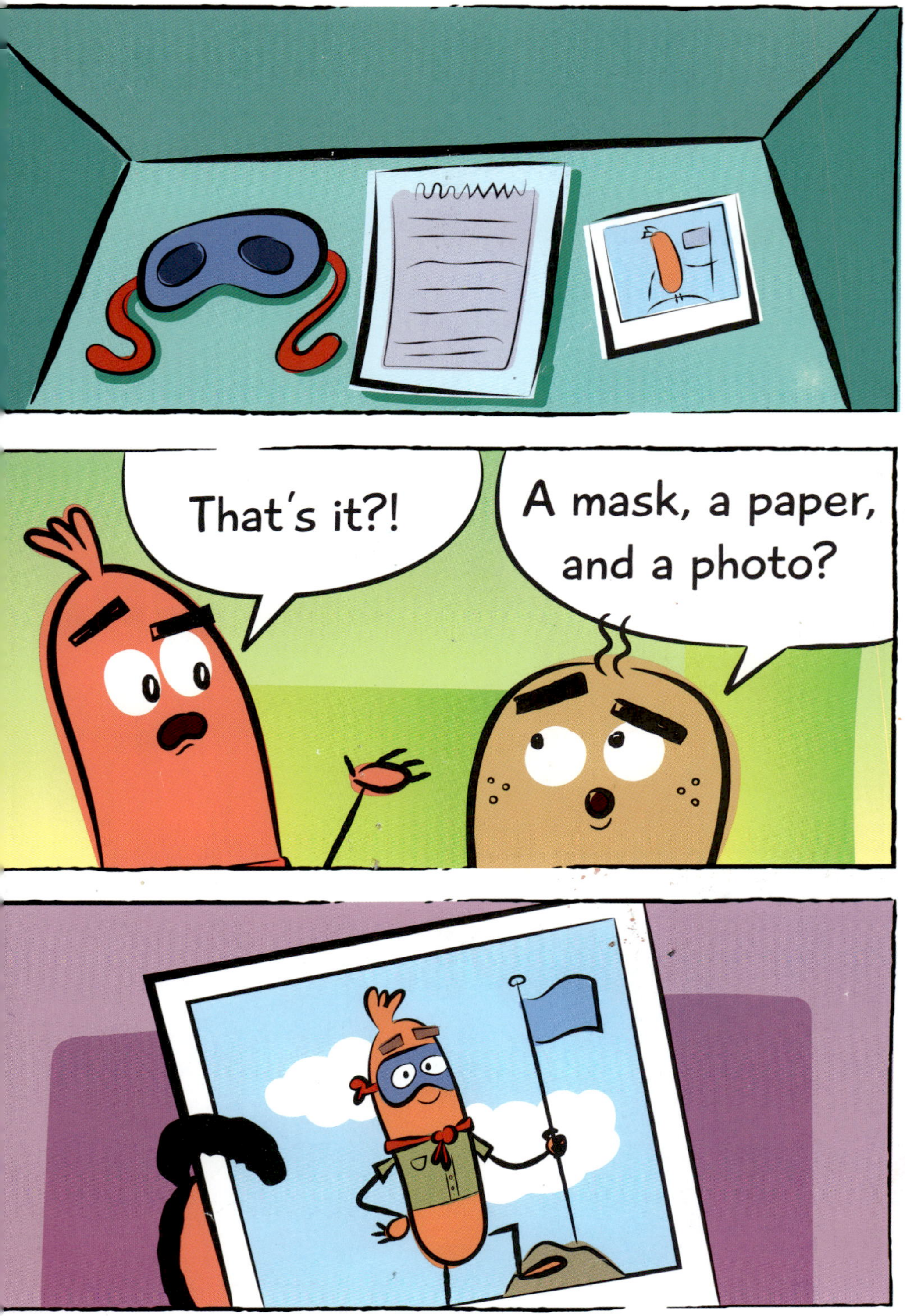
That's it?!
A mask, a paper, and a photo?

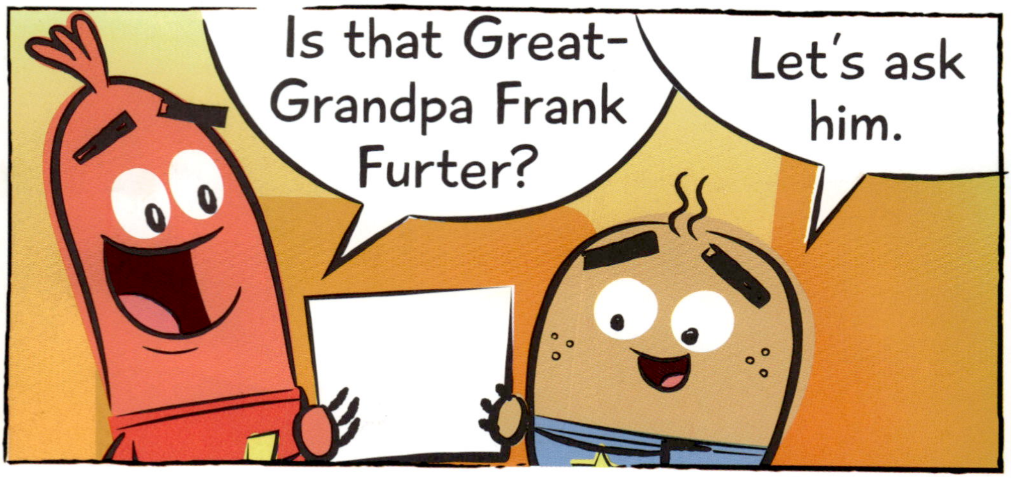
Is that Great-Grandpa Frank Furter?
Let's ask him.

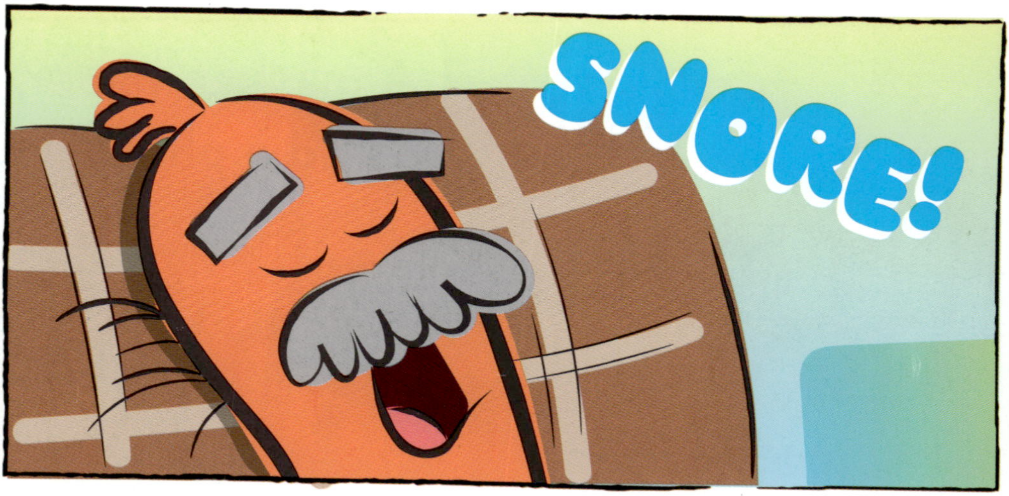
SNORE!

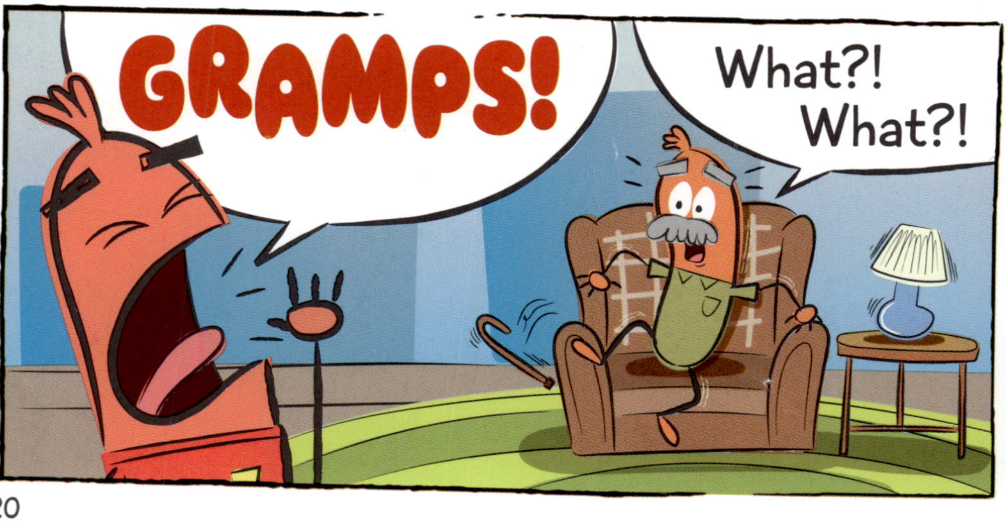
GRAMPS!
What?! What?!

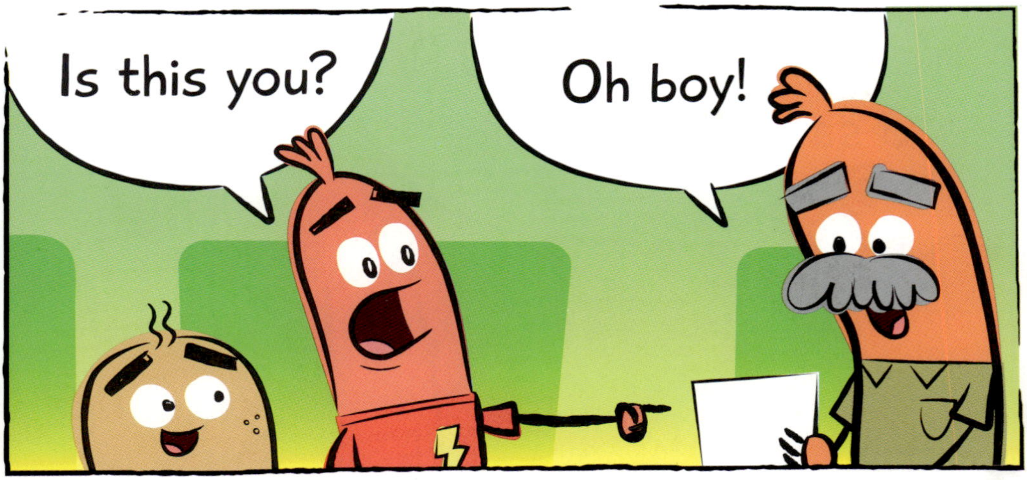
Is this you?
Oh boy!

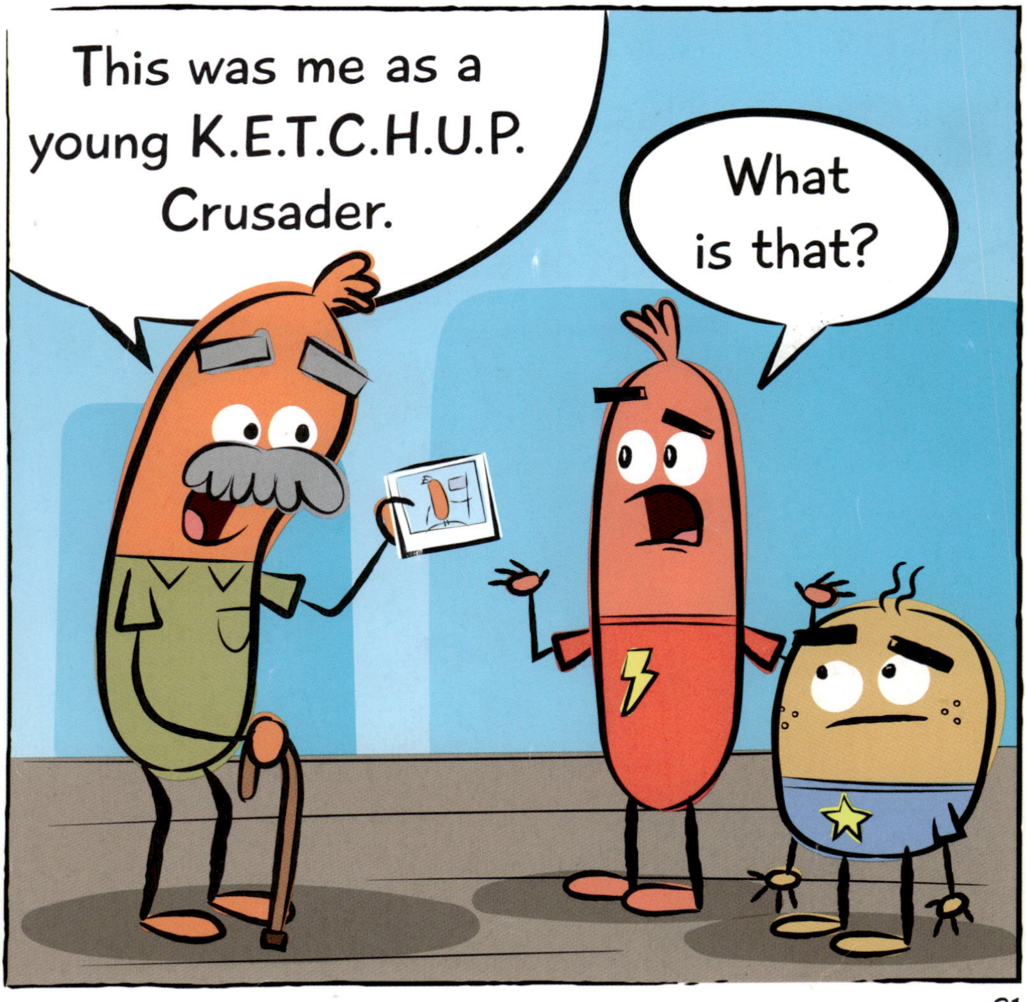
This was me as a young K.E.T.C.H.U.P. Crusader.
What is that?

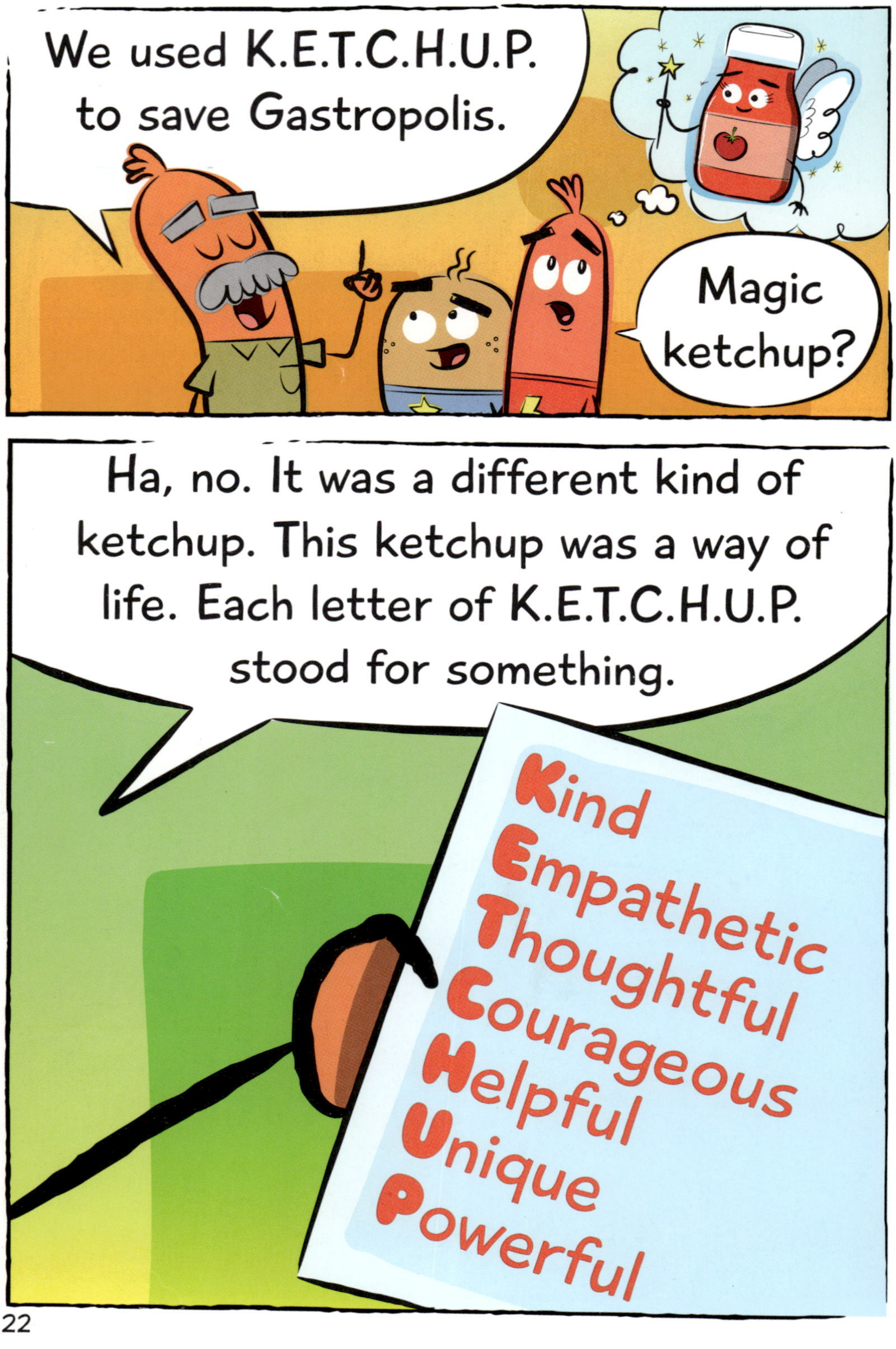
We used K.E.T.C.H.U.P. to save Gastropolis.
Magic ketchup?
Ha, no. It was a different kind of ketchup. This ketchup was a way of life. Each letter of K.E.T.C.H.U.P. stood for something.
Kind
Empathetic
Thoughtful
Courageous
Helpful
Unique
Powerful

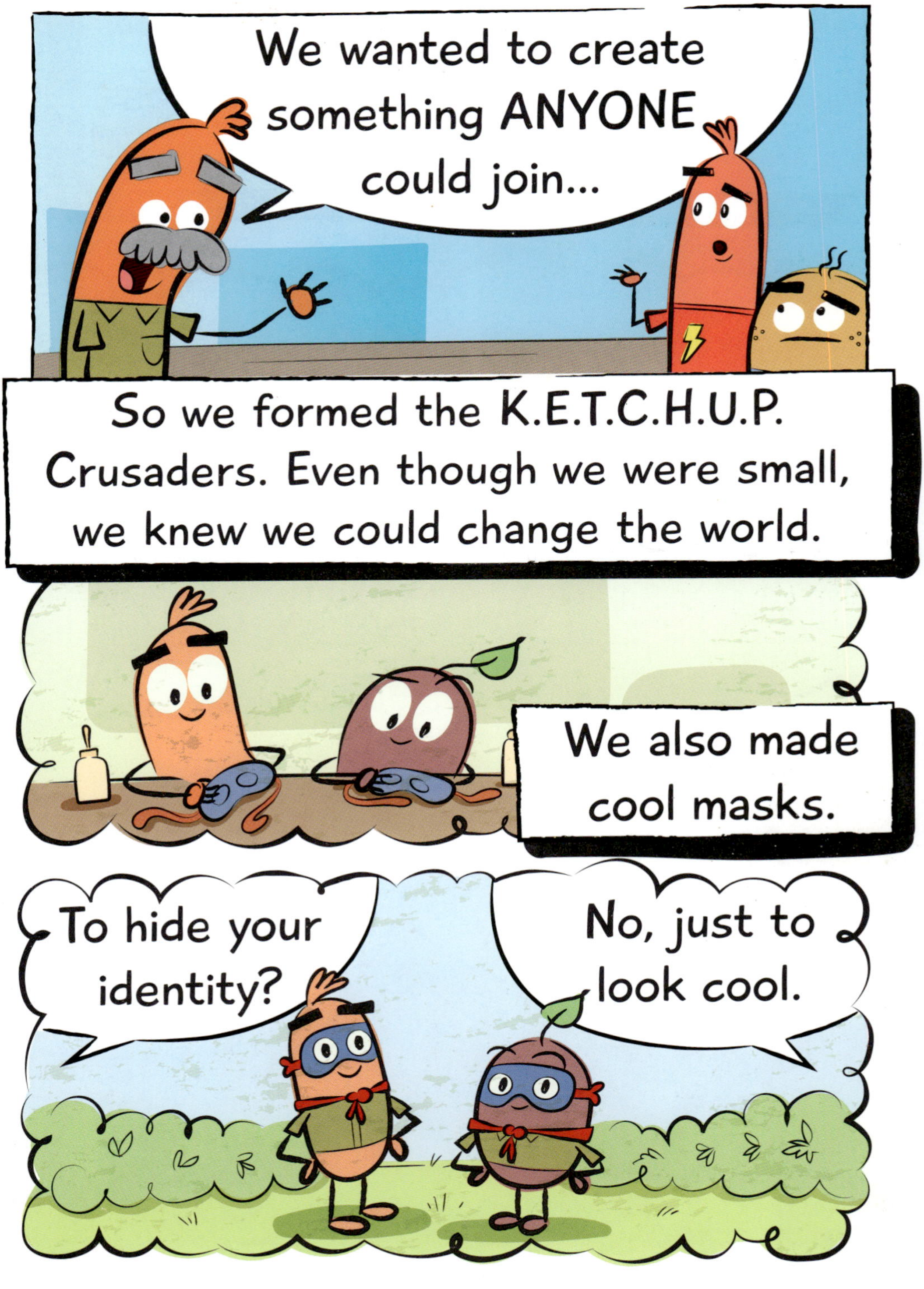
We wanted to create something ANYONE could join...
So we formed the K.E.T.C.H.U.P. Crusaders. Even though we were small, we knew we could change the world.
We also made cool masks.
To hide your identity?
No, just to look cool.

One day we found out that someone named Mayo Naze was making evil plans.

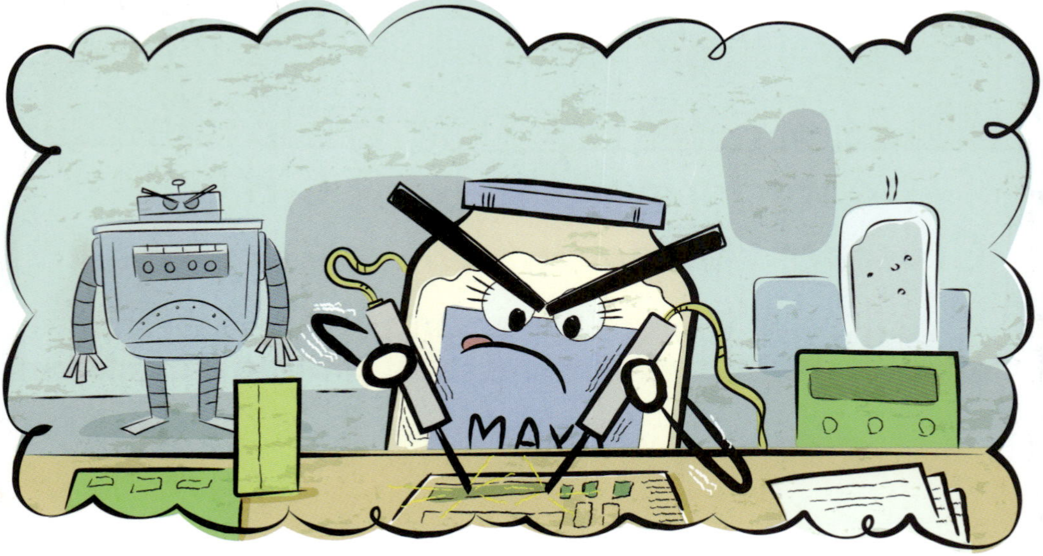
MAYO

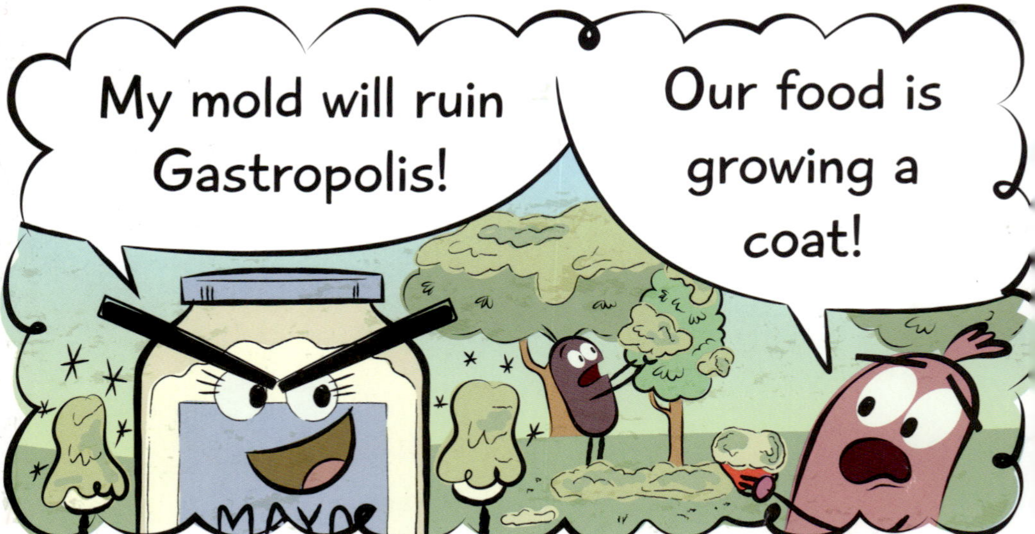
My mold will ruin Gastropolis!
Our food is growing a coat!
MAYO

Through the power of K.E.T.C.H.U.P., we began to ruin Mayo Naze's plans by being so kind to her that she forgot to be mean.

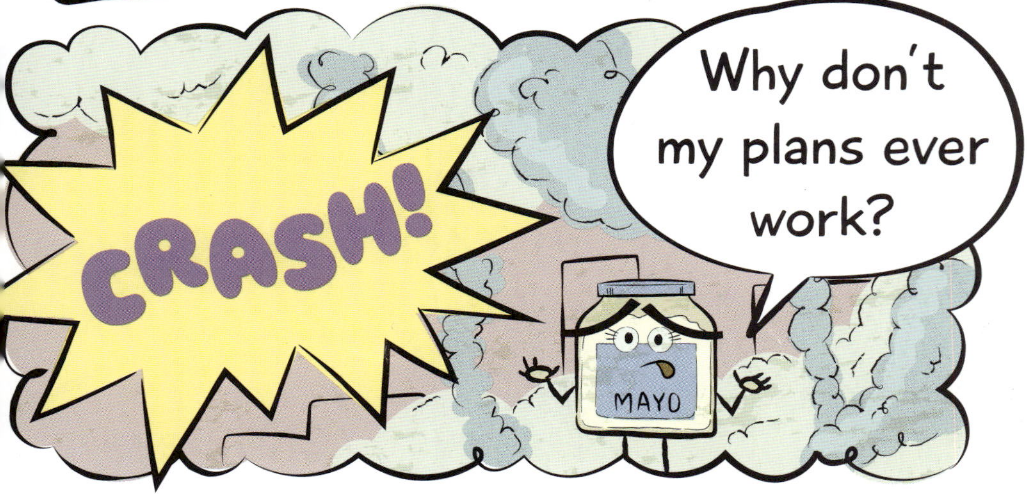
CRASH!
Why don't my plans ever work?
MAYO

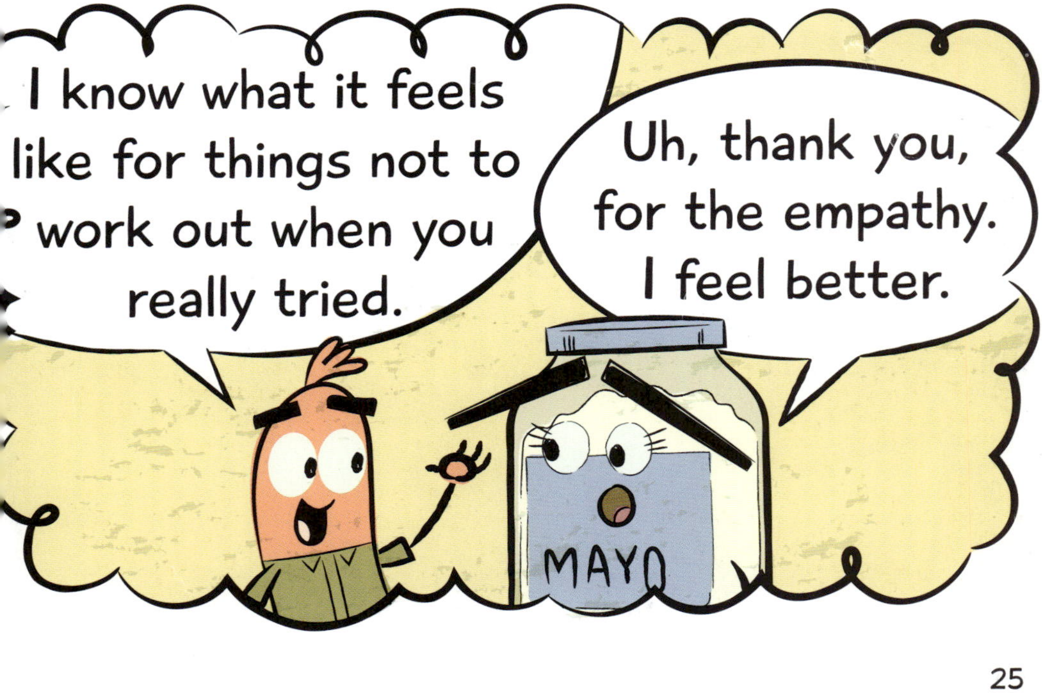
I know what it feels like for things not to work out when you really tried.
Uh, thank you, for the empathy. I feel better.
MAYO

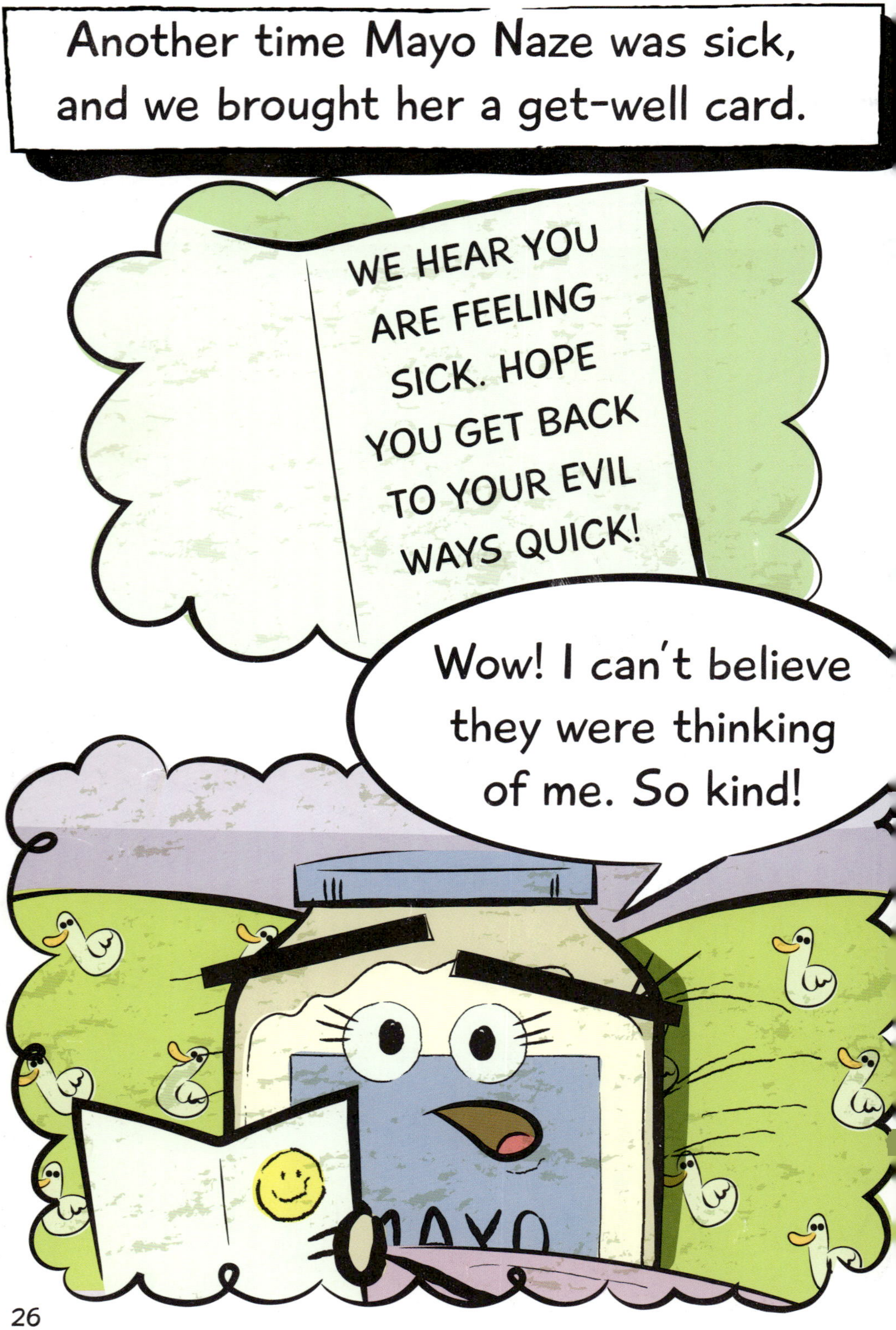
Another time Mayo Naze was sick, and we brought her a get-well card.
WE HEAR YOU ARE FEELING SICK. HOPE YOU GET BACK TO YOUR EVIL WAYS QUICK!
Wow! I can't believe they were thinking of me. So kind!
MAYO

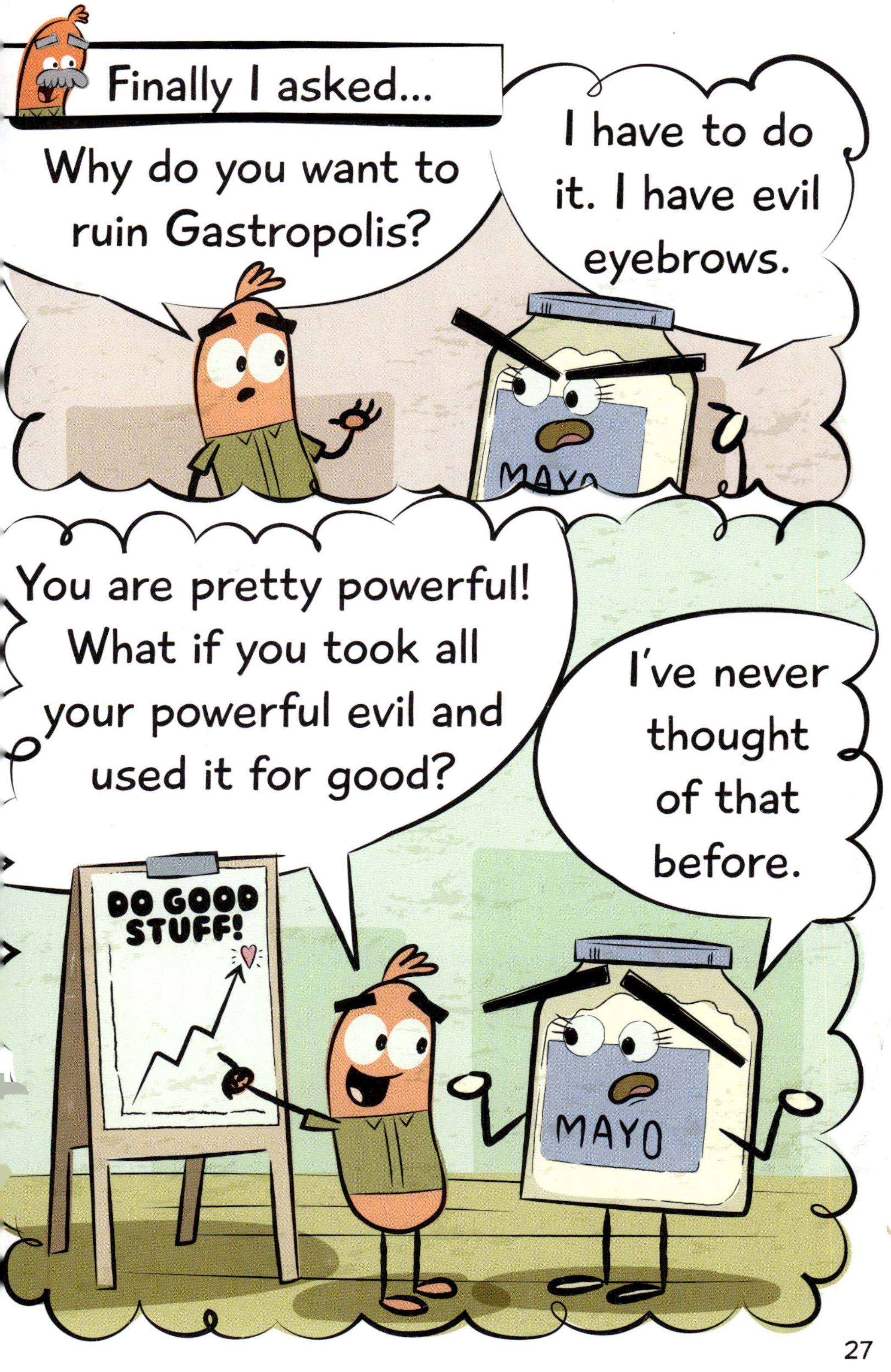
Finally I asked...
Why do you want to ruin Gastropolis?
I have to do it. I have evil eyebrows.
MAYO
You are pretty powerful! What if you took all your powerful evil and used it for good?
I've never thought of that before.
DO GOOD STUFF!
MAYO

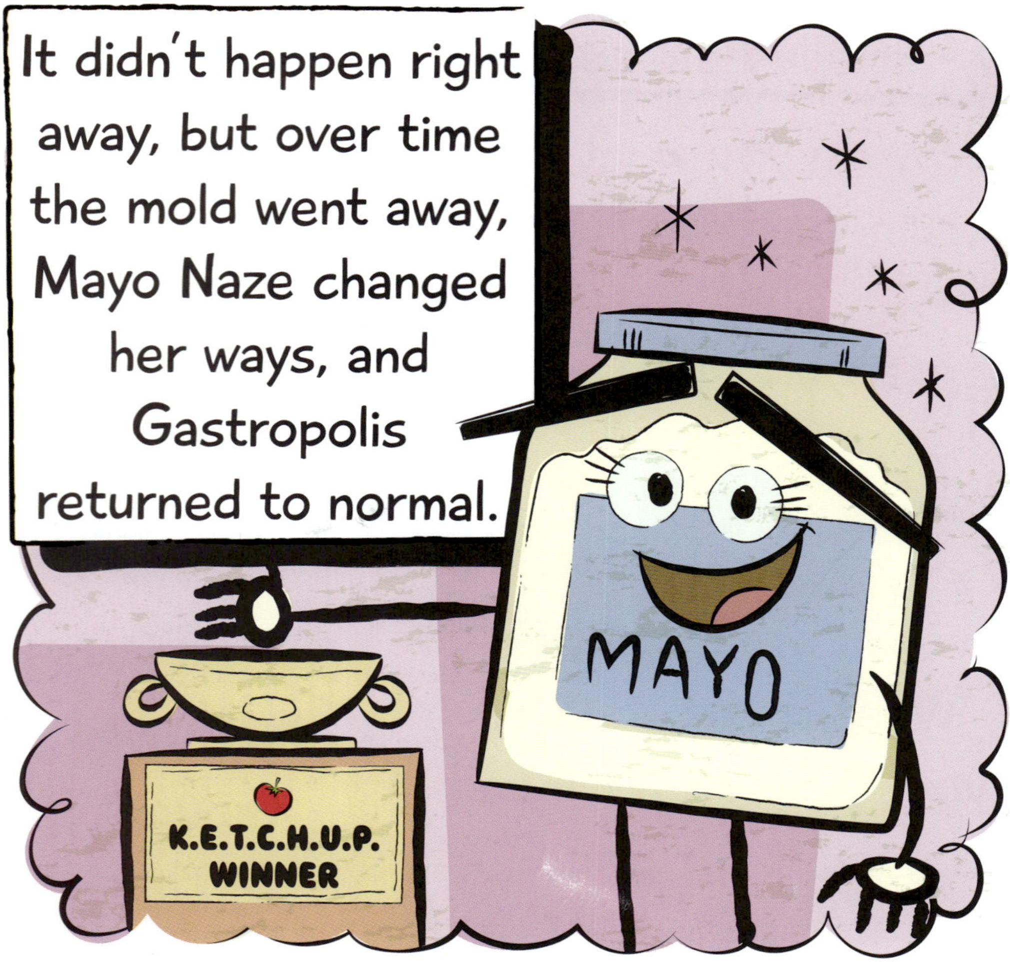
It didn't happen right away, but over time the mold went away, Mayo Naze changed her ways, and Gastropolis returned to normal.
K.E.T.C.H.U.P. WINNER
MAYO

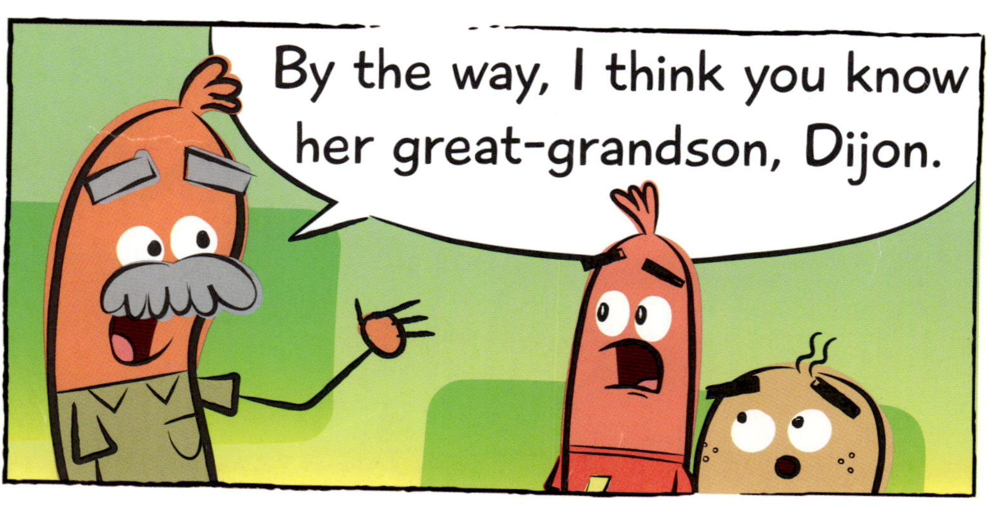
By the way, I think you know her great-grandson, Dijon.

Chapter 4
WE ALL SCREAM!

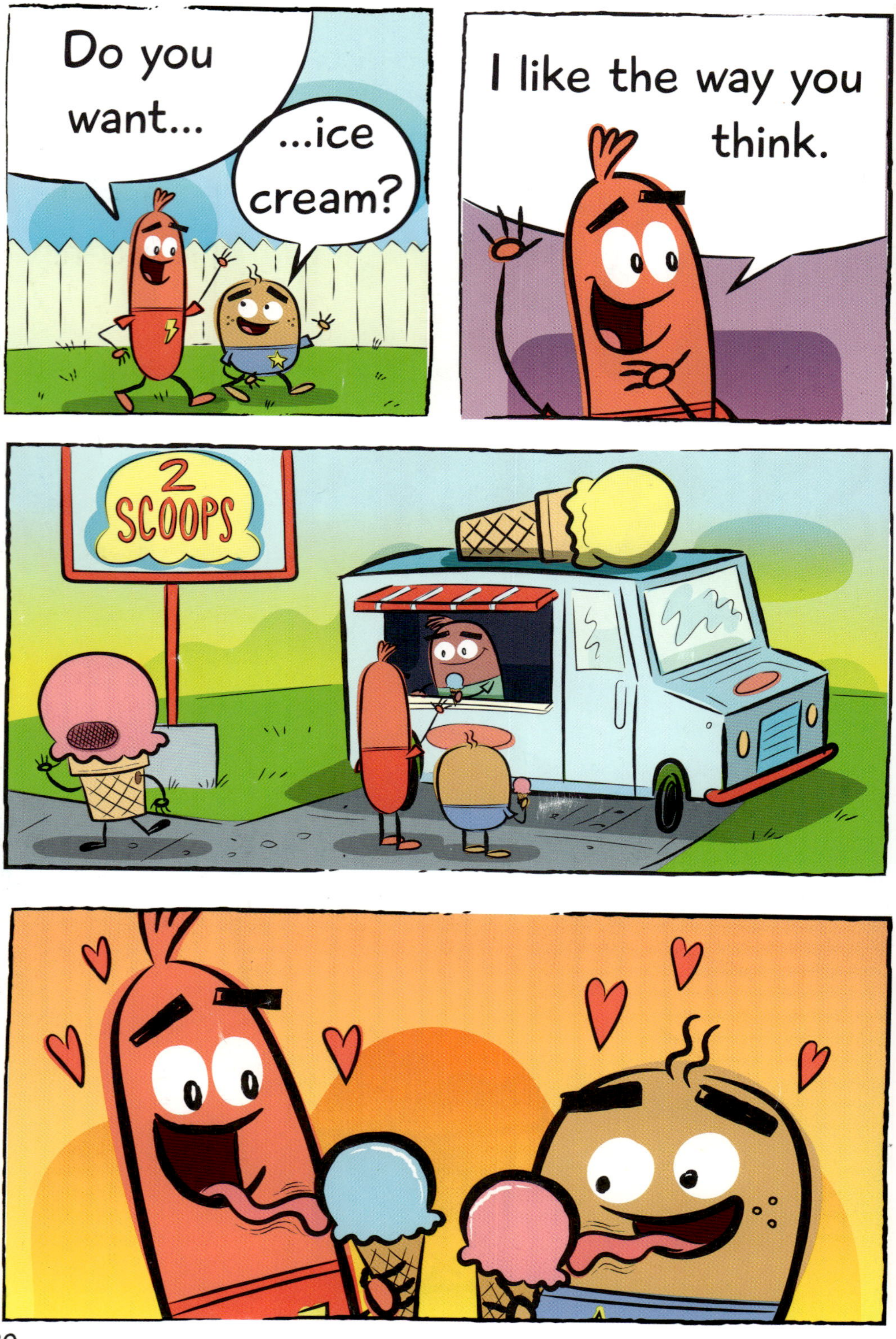
Do you want...
...ice cream?
I like the way you think.
2 SCOOPS

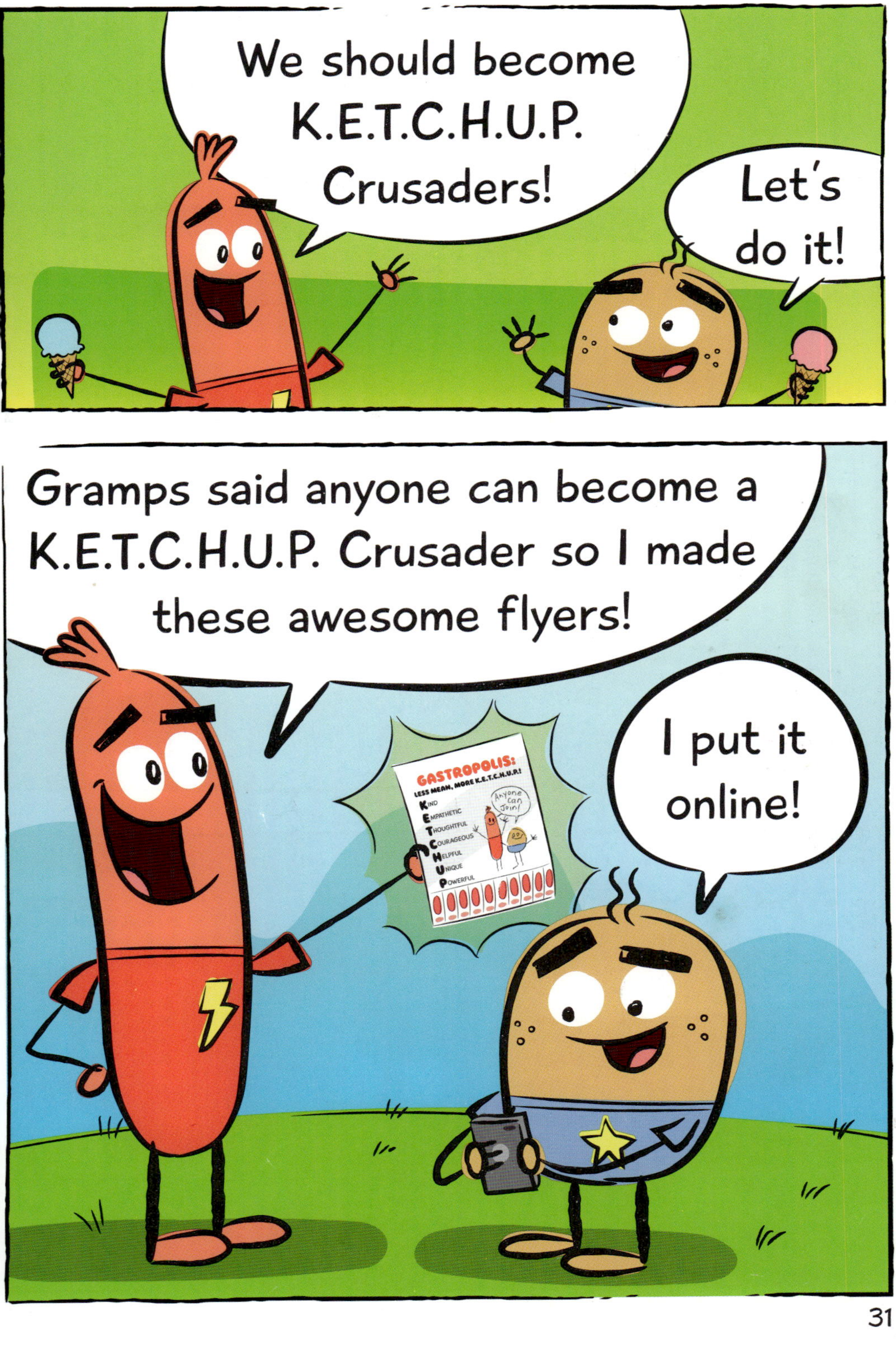
We should become K.E.T.C.H.U.P. Crusaders!
Let's do it!
Gramps said anyone can become a K.E.T.C.H.U.P. Crusader so I made these awesome flyers!
GASTROPOLIS:
LESS MEAN, MORE K.E.T.C.H.U.P.!
KIND
EMPATHETIC
THOUGHTFUL
COURAGEOUS
HELPFUL
UNIQUE
POWERFUL
Anyone can Join!
I put it online!

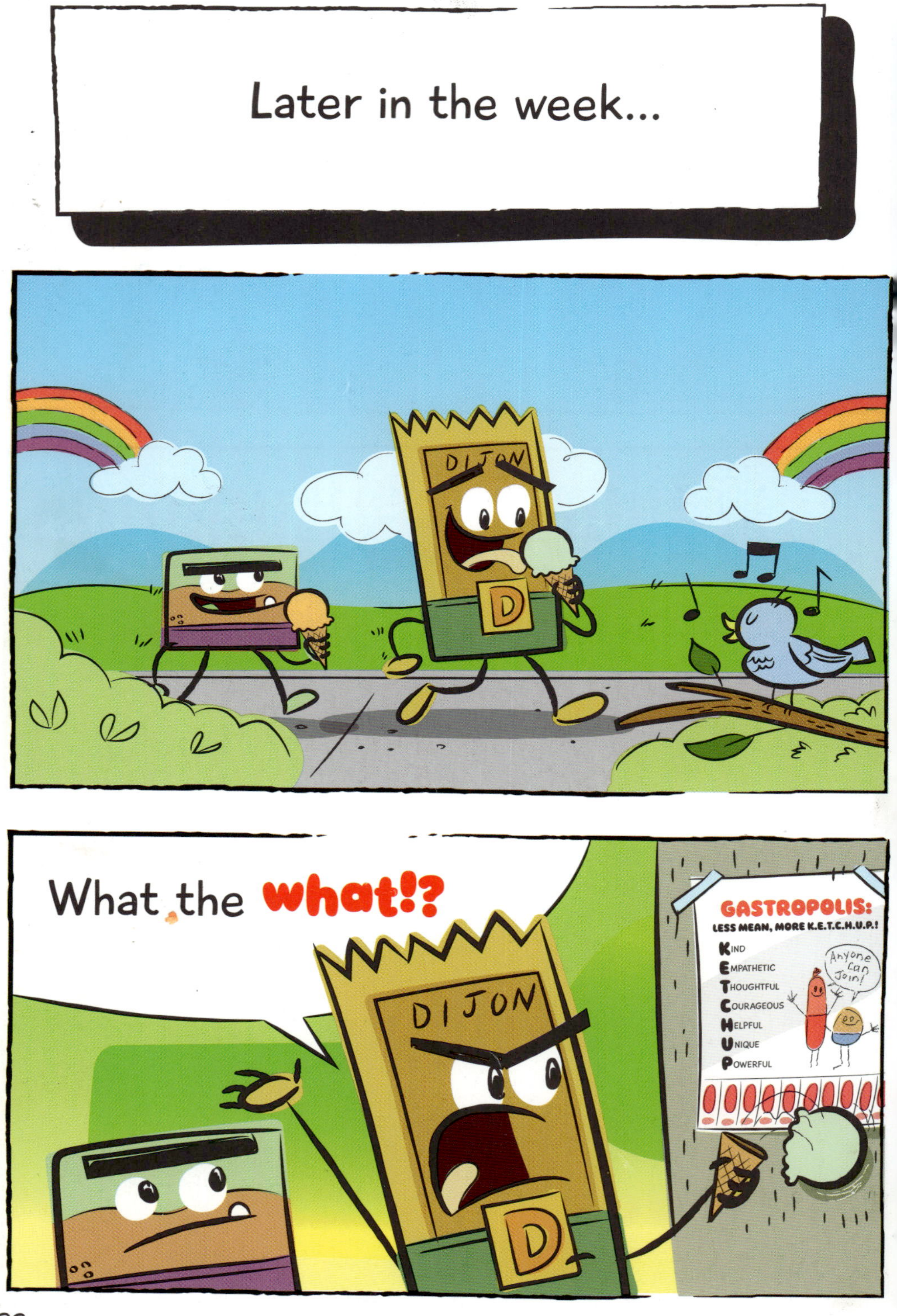
Later in the week...
DIJON
D
What the what!?
DIJON
D
GASTROPOLIS:
LESS MEAN, MORE K.E.T.C.H.U.P.!
KIND
EMPATHETIC
THOUGHTFUL
COURAGEOUS
HELPFUL
UNIQUE
POWERFUL
Anyone can Join!

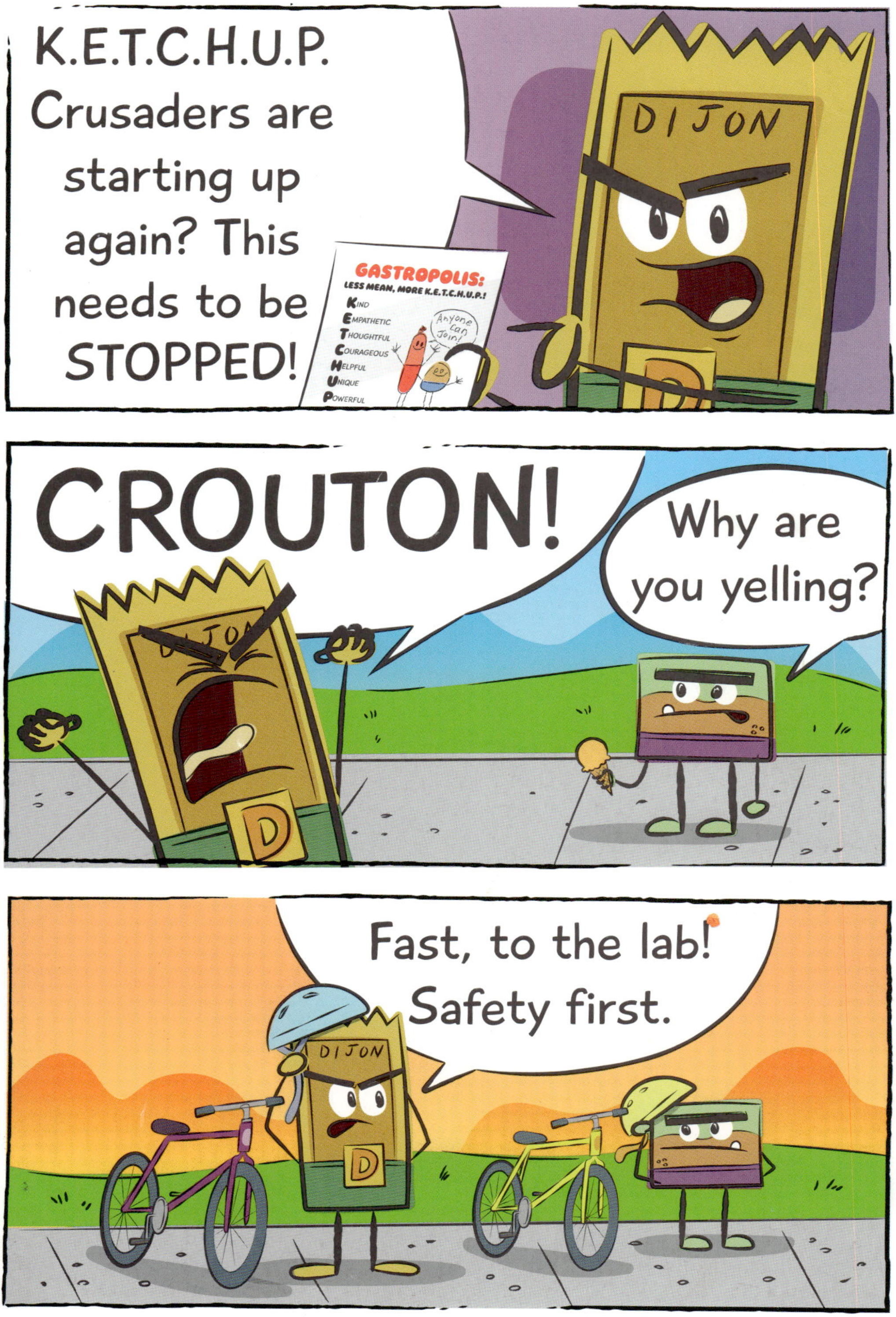
K.E.T.C.H.U.P. Crusaders are starting up again? This needs to be STOPPED!
GASTROPOLIS:
LESS MEAN, MORE K.E.T.C.H.U.P.!
KIND
EMPATHETIC
THOUGHTFUL
COURAGEOUS
HELPFUL
UNIQUE
POWERFUL
Anyone can join!
DIJON
CROUTON!
Why are you yelling?
Fast, to the lab! Safety first.

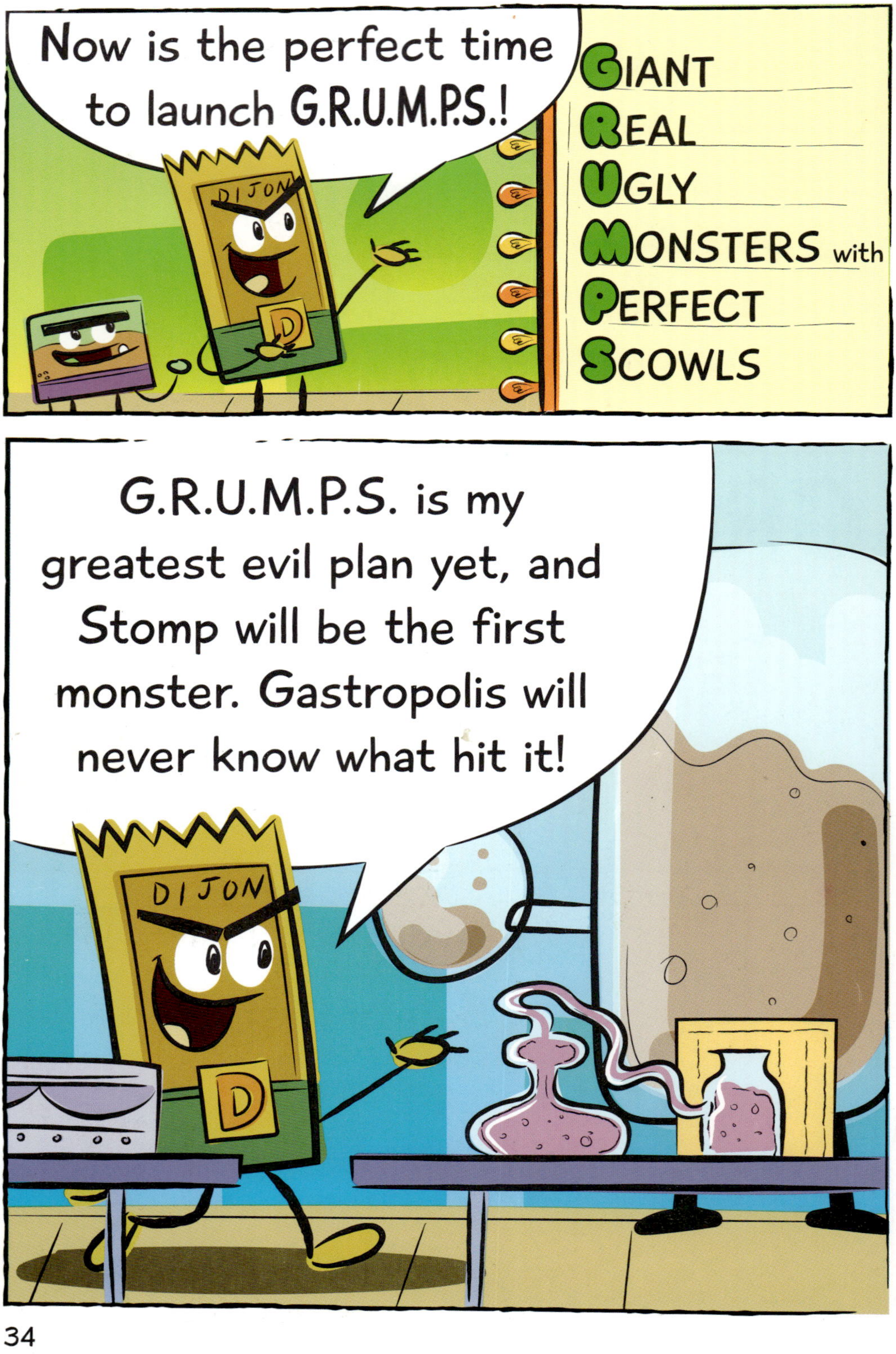
Now is the perfect time to launch G.R.U.M.P.S.!
GIANT
REAL
UGLY
MONSTERS with
PERFECT
SCOWLS
DIJON
D
G.R.U.M.P.S. is my greatest evil plan yet, and Stomp will be the first monster. Gastropolis will never know what hit it!
DIJON
D

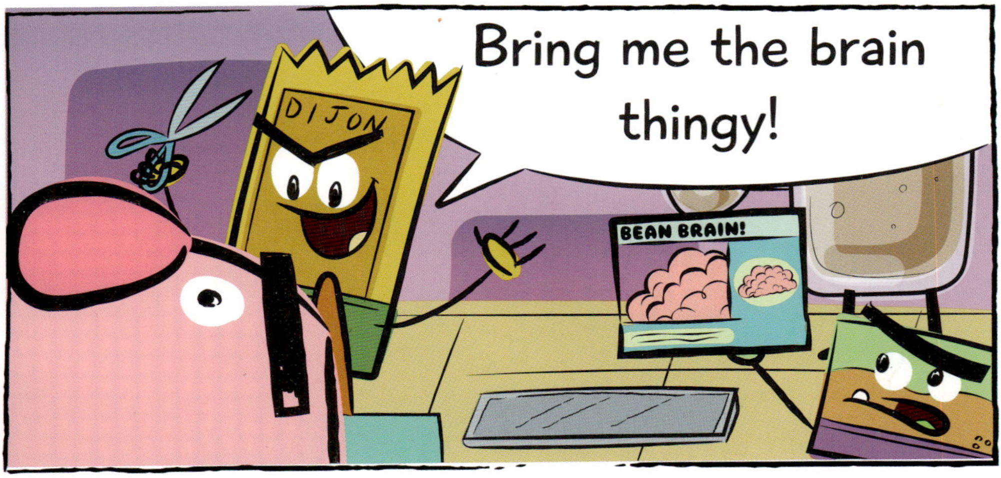
Bring me the brain thingy!
DIJON
BEAN BRAIN!

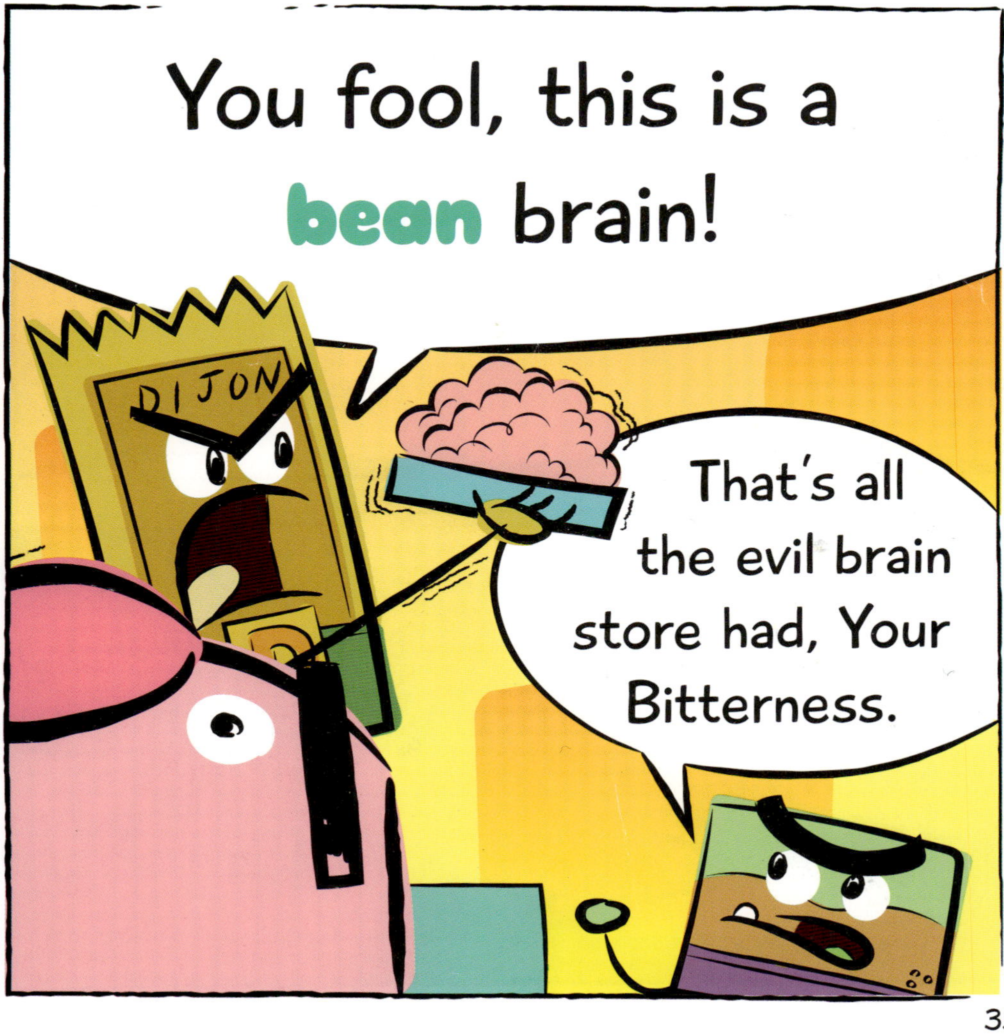
You fool, this is a bean brain!
DIJON
That's all the evil brain store had, Your Bitterness.

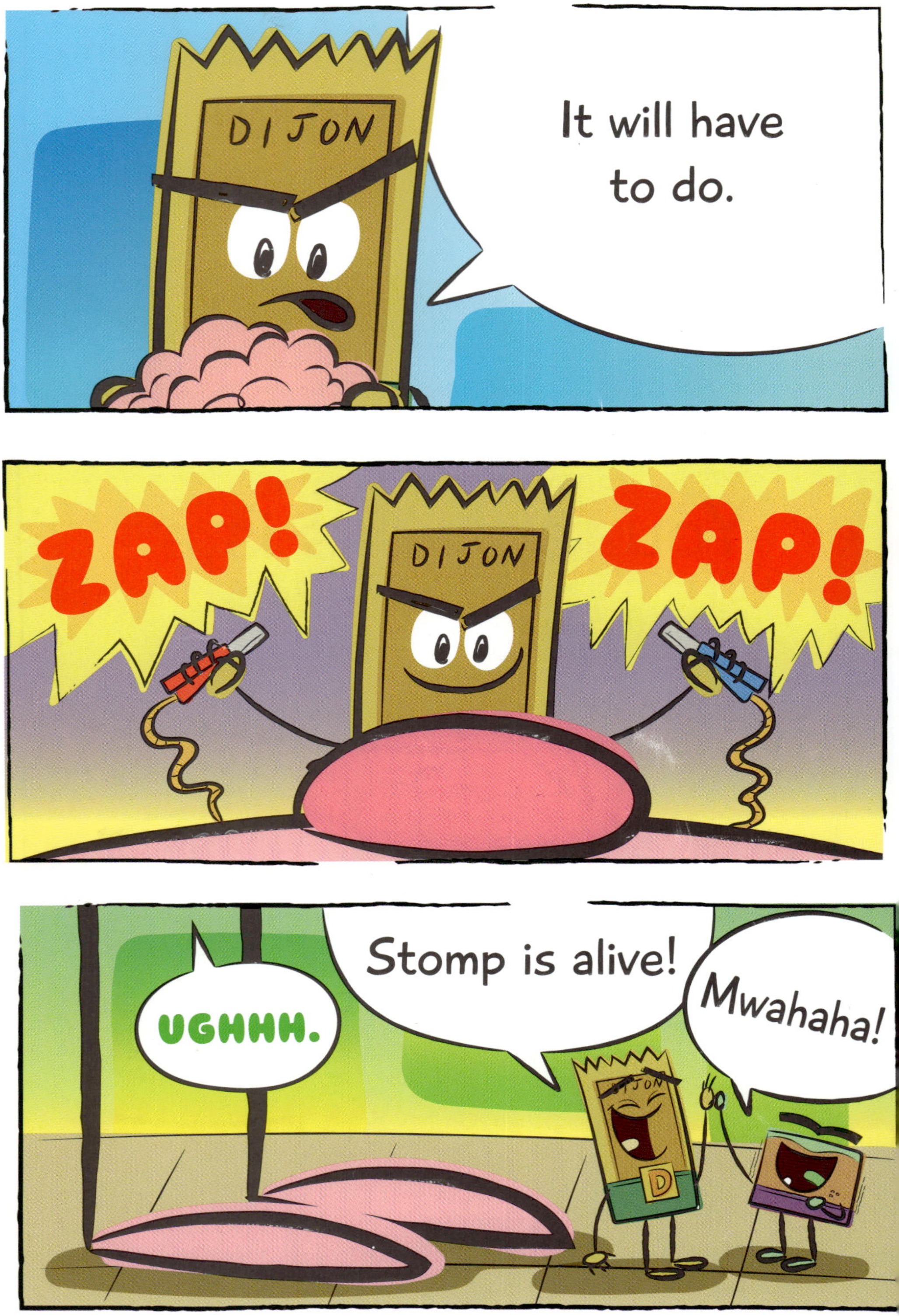
DIJON
It will have to do.
ZAP!
ZAP!
DIJON
UGHHH.
Stomp is alive!
Mwahaha!
D

Chapter 5

NO BRAINER!

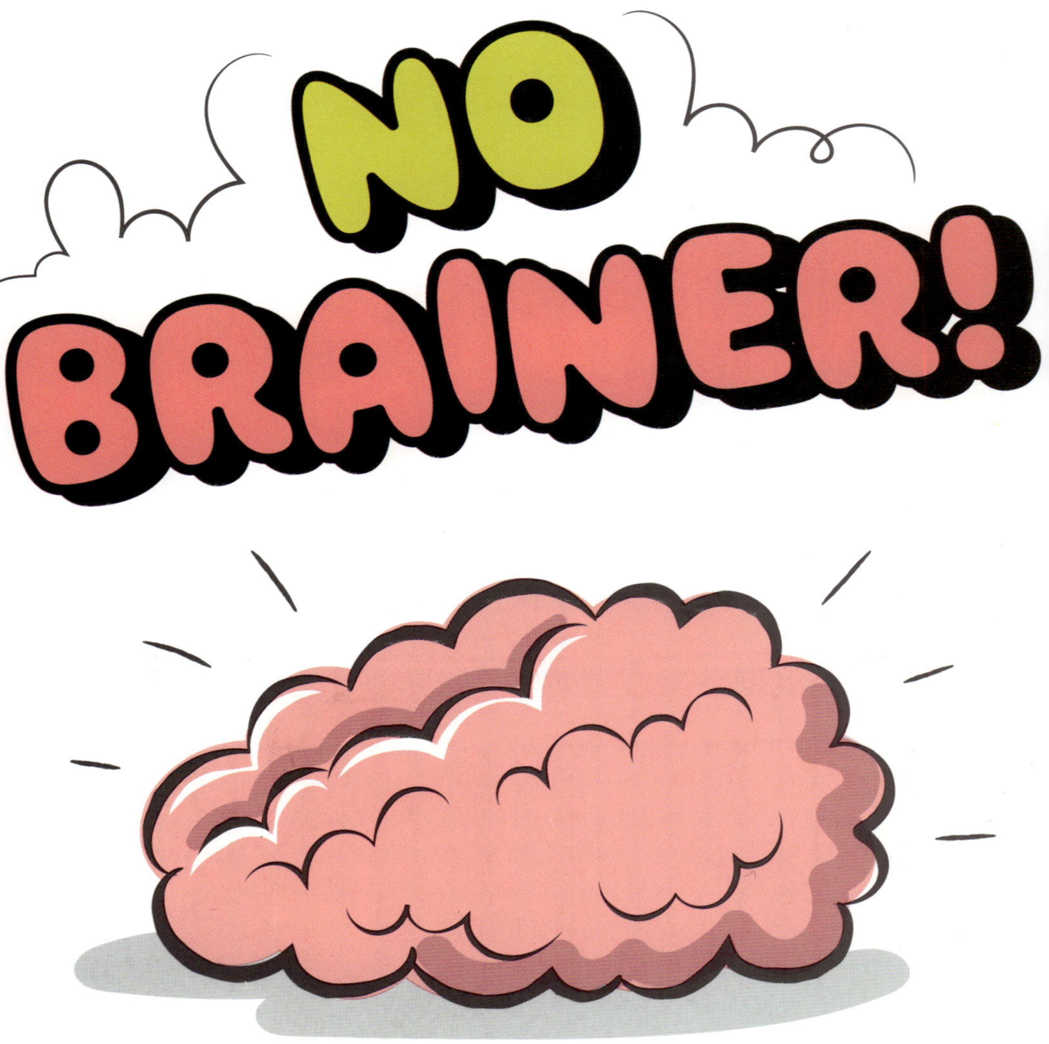

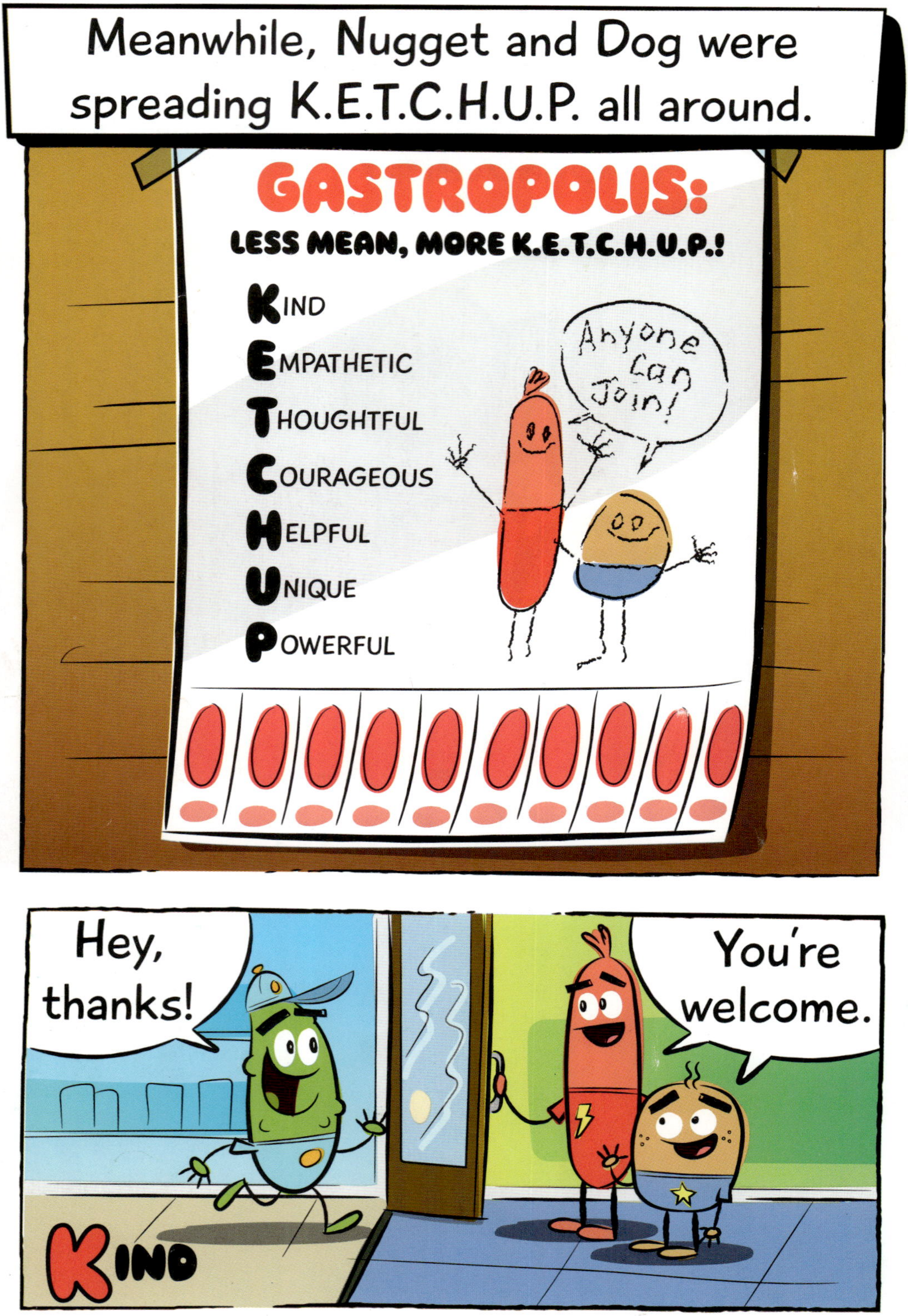
Meanwhile, Nugget and Dog were spreading K.E.T.C.H.U.P. all around.
GASTROPOLIS:
LESS MEAN, MORE K.E.T.C.H.U.P.!
KIND
EMPATHETIC
THOUGHTFUL
COURAGEOUS
HELPFUL
UNIQUE
POWERFUL
Anyone can Join!
Hey, thanks!
You're welcome.
KIND

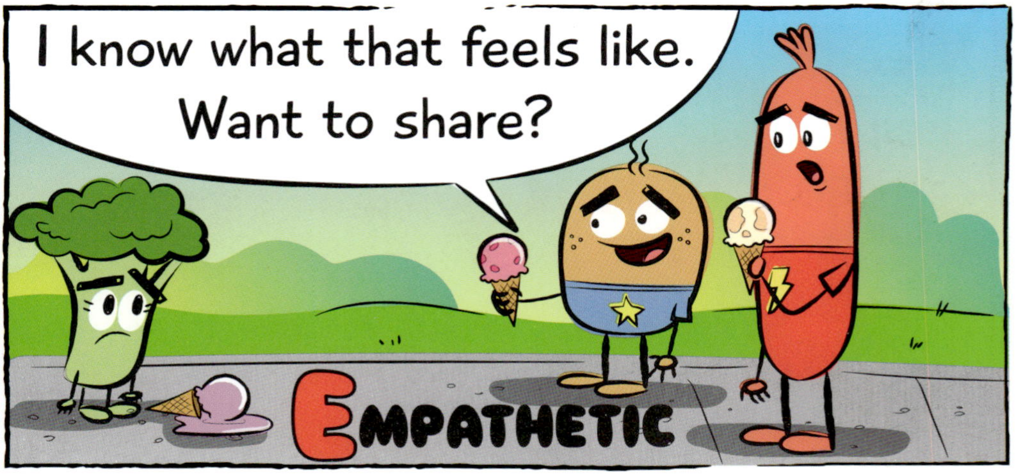
I know what that feels like. Want to share?
EMPATHETIC

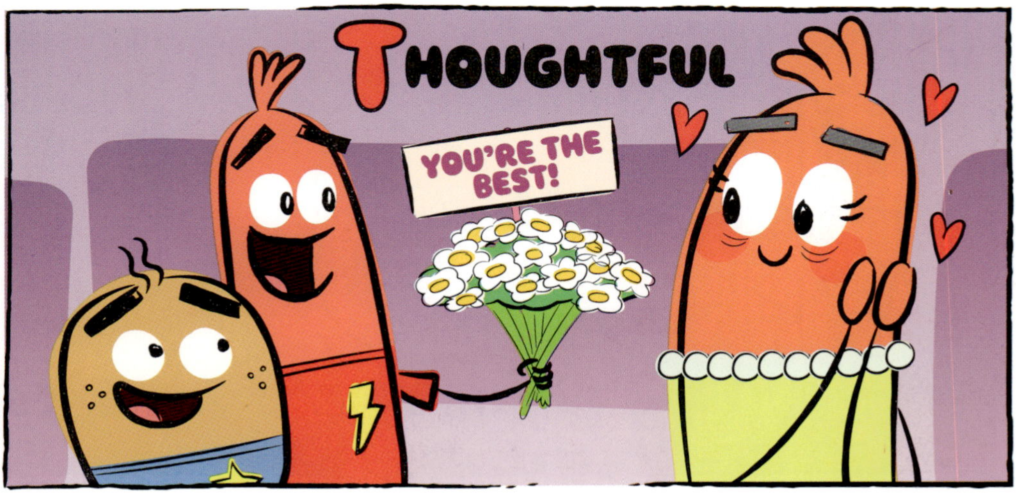
THOUGHTFUL
YOU'RE THE BEST!

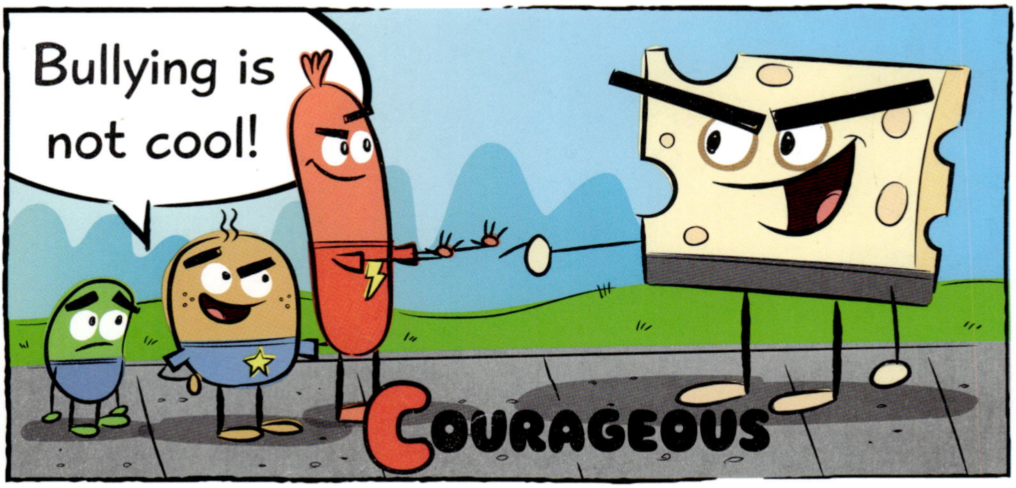
Bullying is not cool!
COURAGEOUS

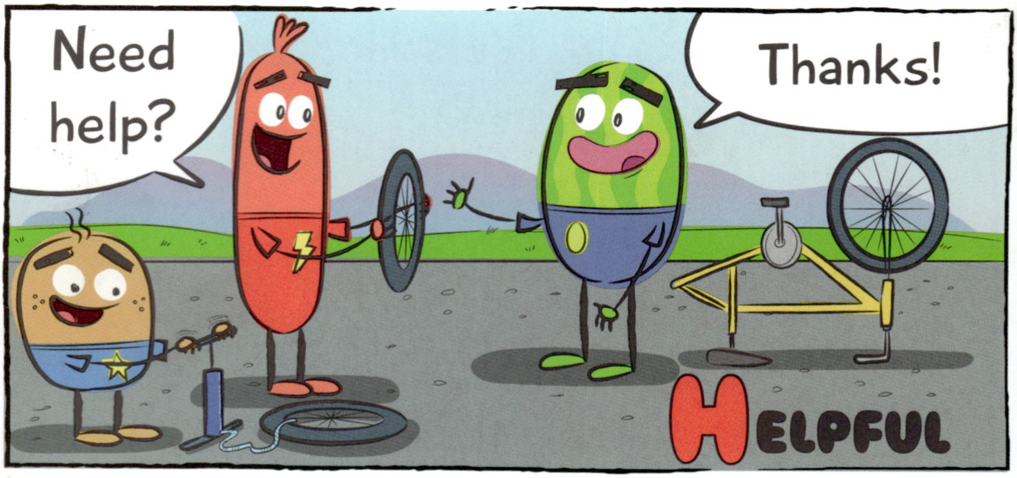
Need help?
Thanks!
HELPFUL

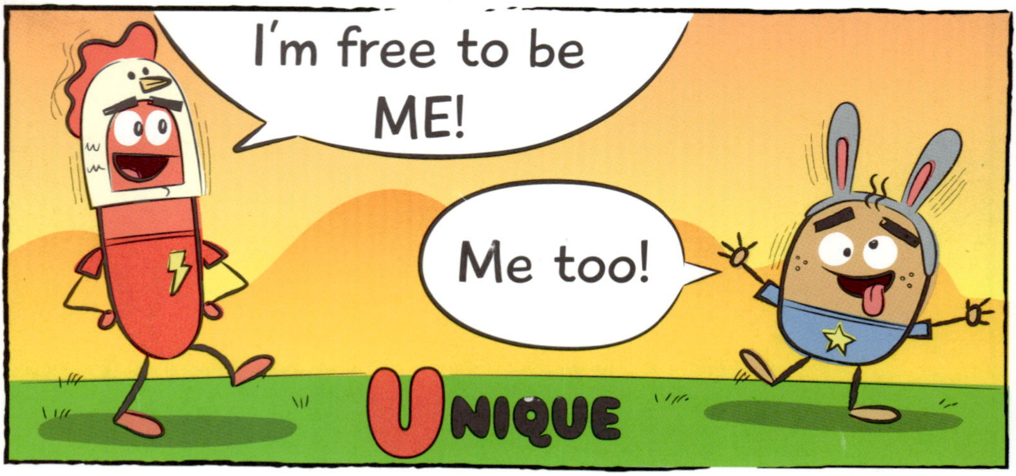
I'm free to be ME!
Me too!
UNIQUE

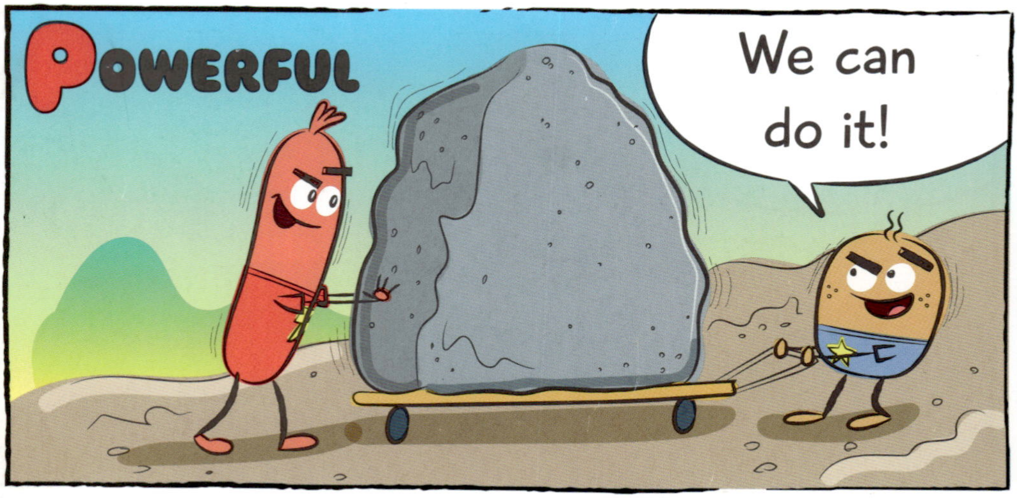
POWERFUL
We can do it!

Then one day, they heard a call for help!

HELP!

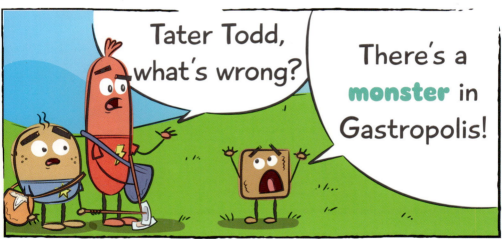

Tater Todd, what's wrong?

There's a **monster** in Gastropolis!

And it wants **brains**!

I **NEED** MY BRAINS!

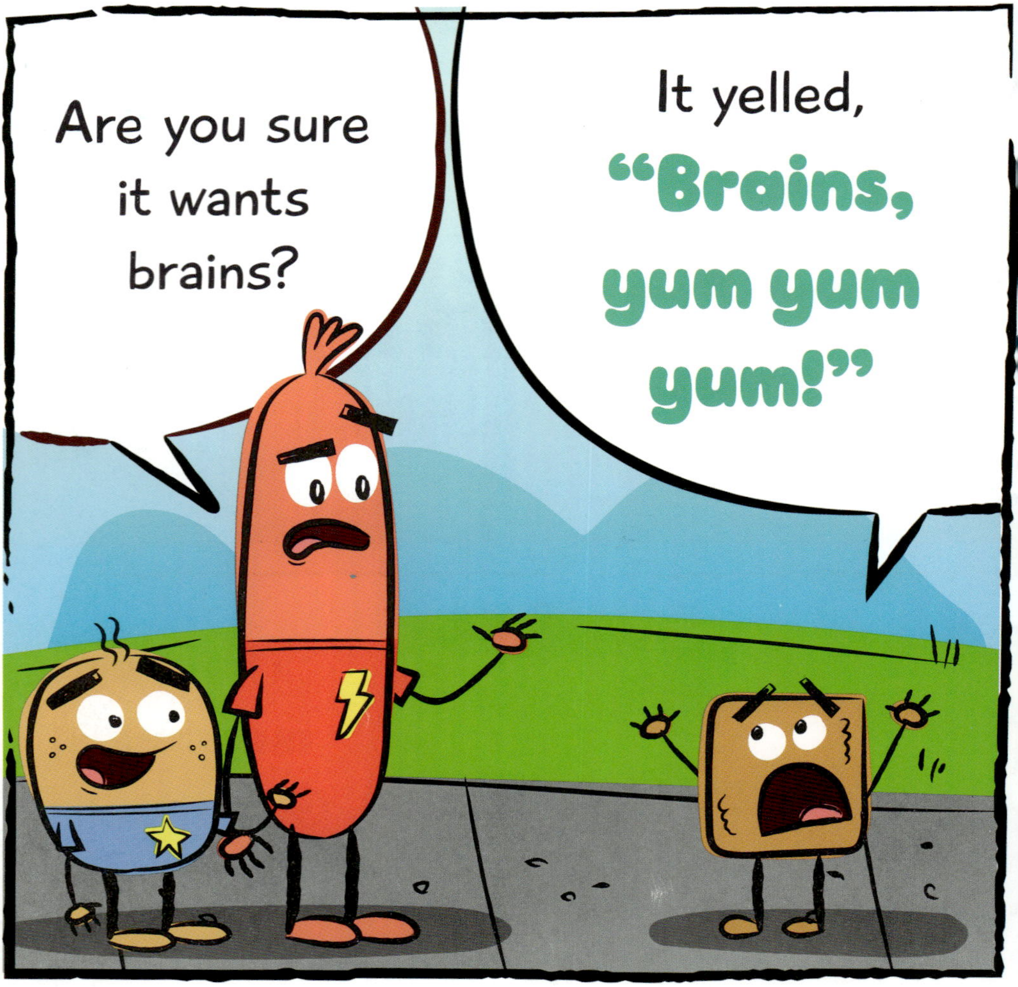
Are you sure it wants brains?
It yelled, "Brains, yum yum yum!"

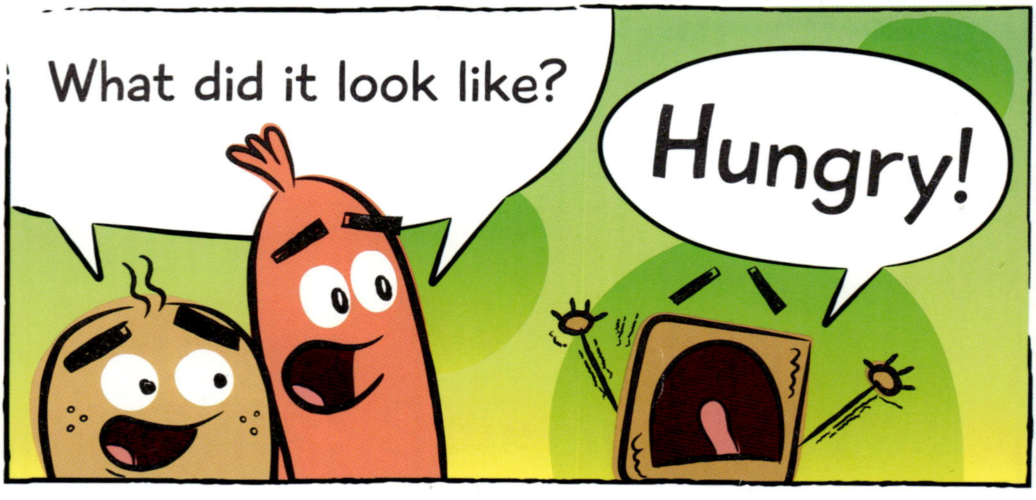
What did it look like?
Hungry!

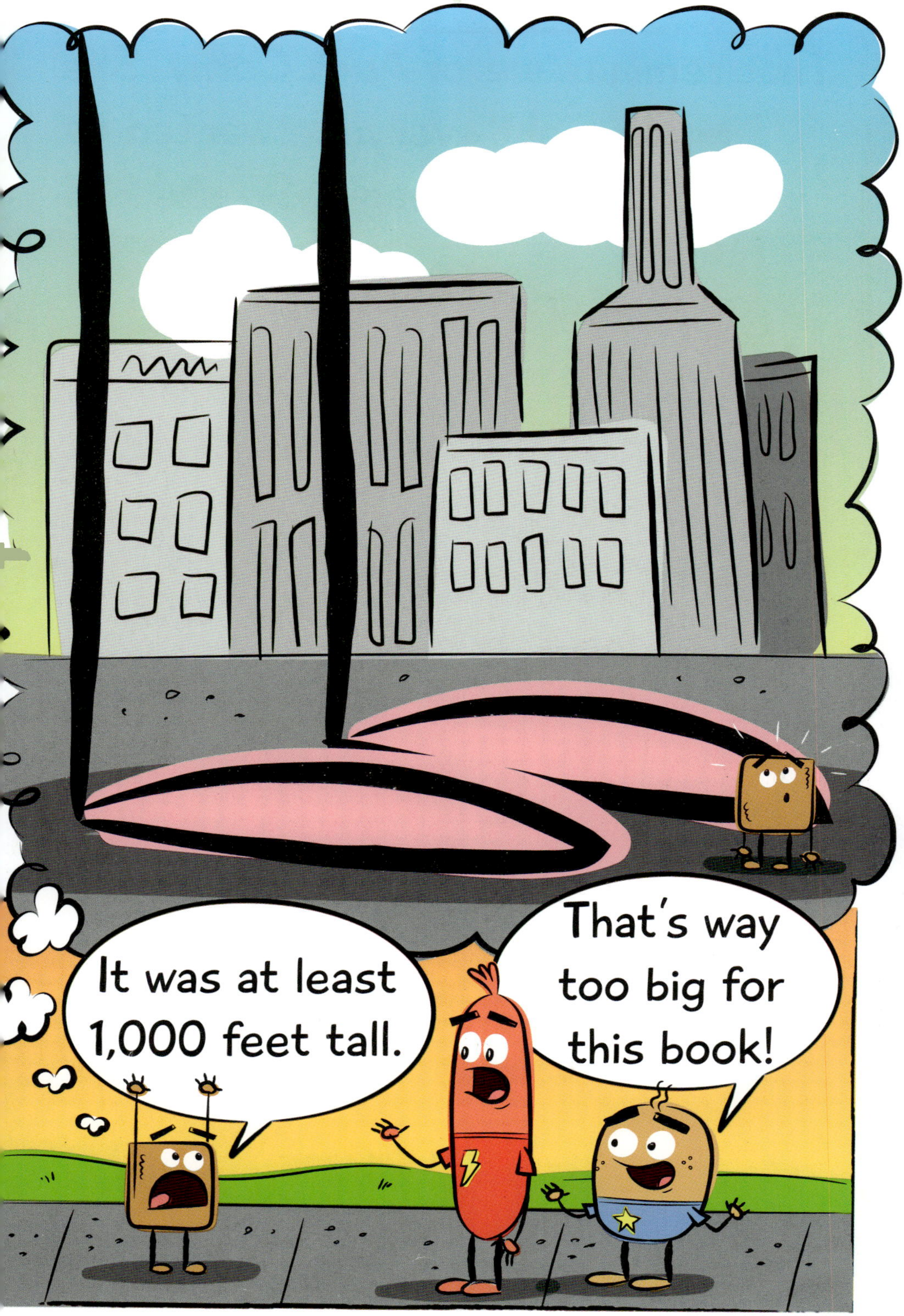
It was at least
1,000 feet tall.
That's way
too big for
this book!

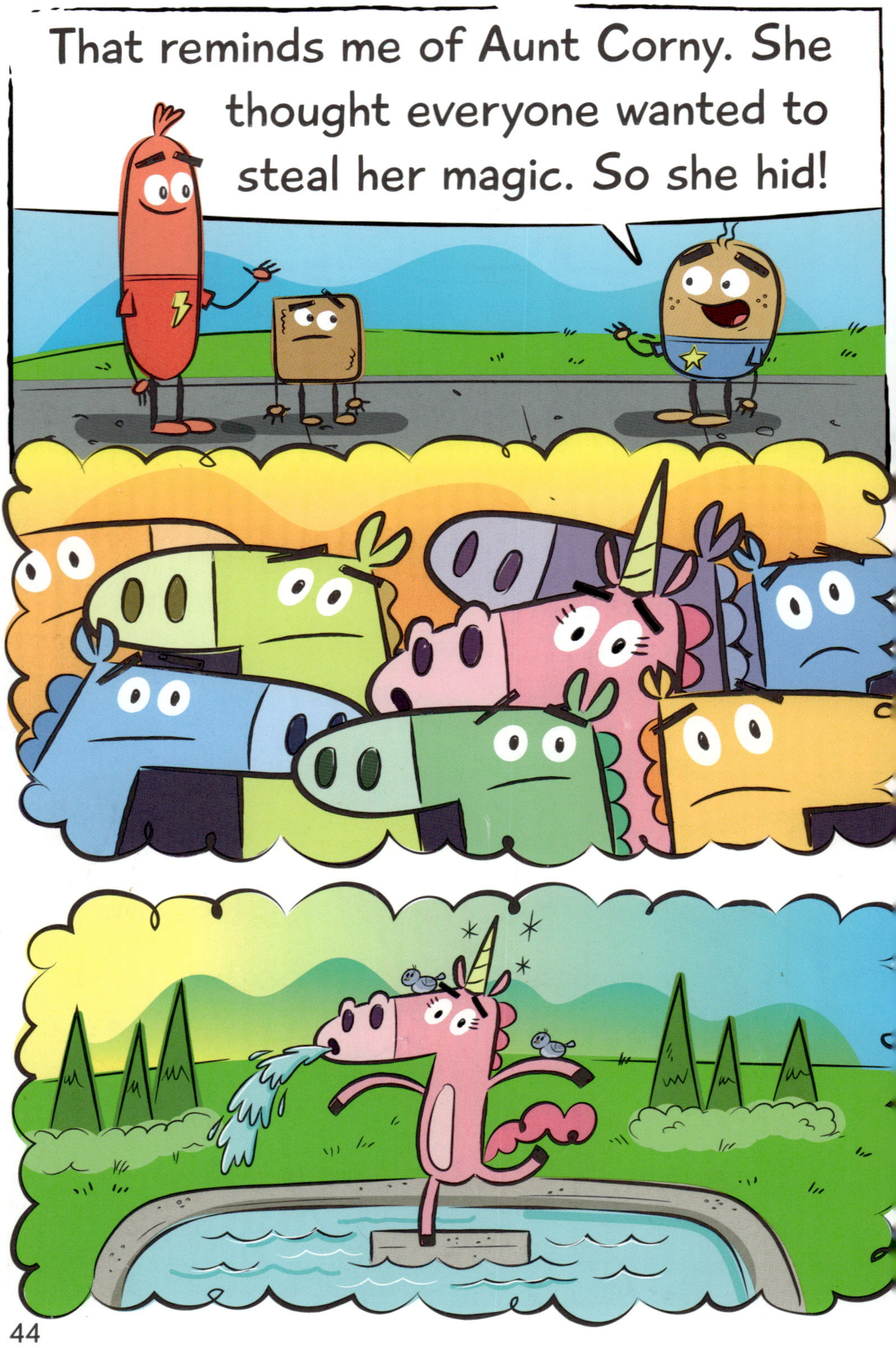
That reminds me of Aunt Corny. She thought everyone wanted to steal her magic. So she hid!

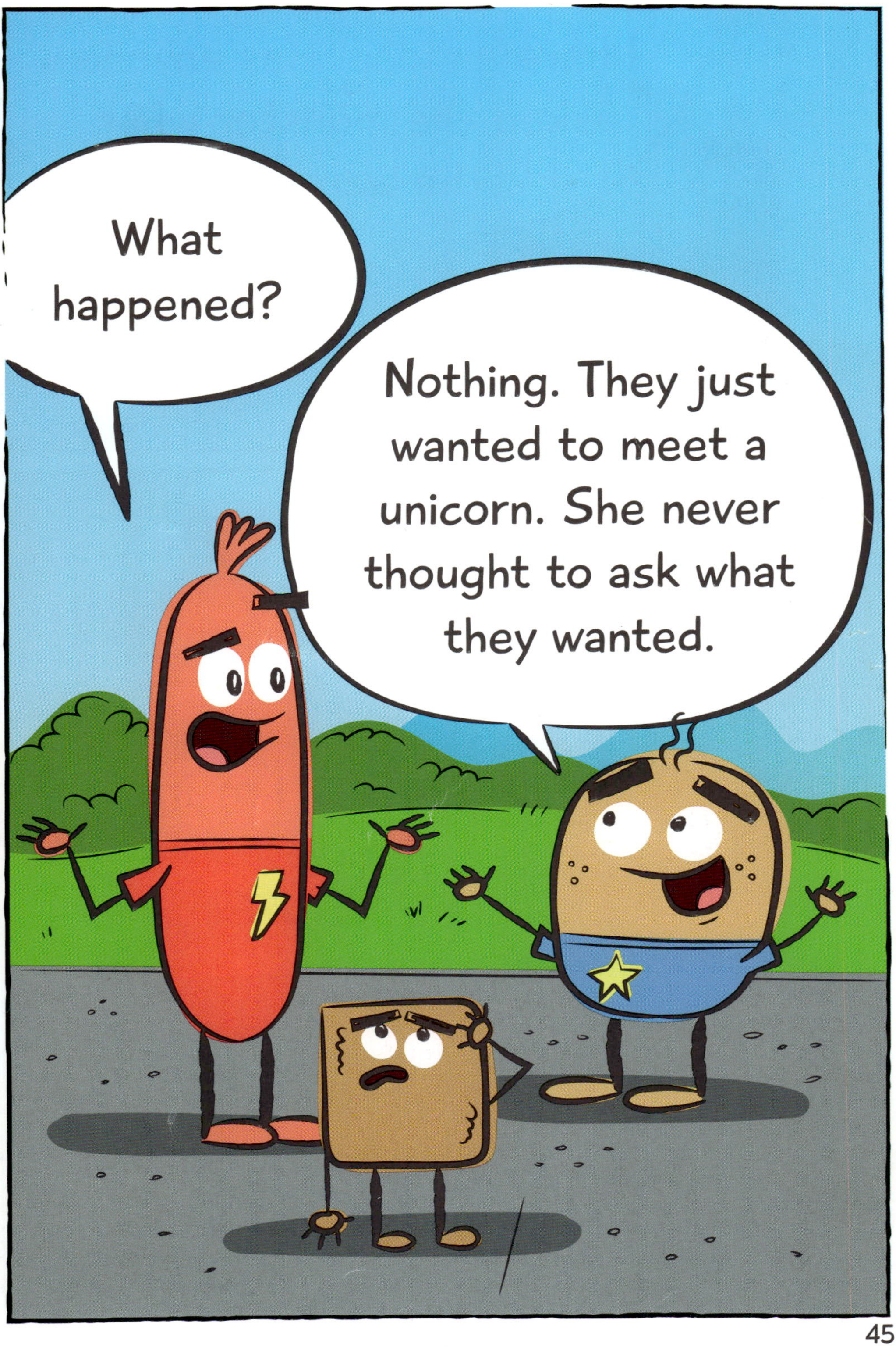
What happened?
Nothing. They just wanted to meet a unicorn. She never thought to ask what they wanted.

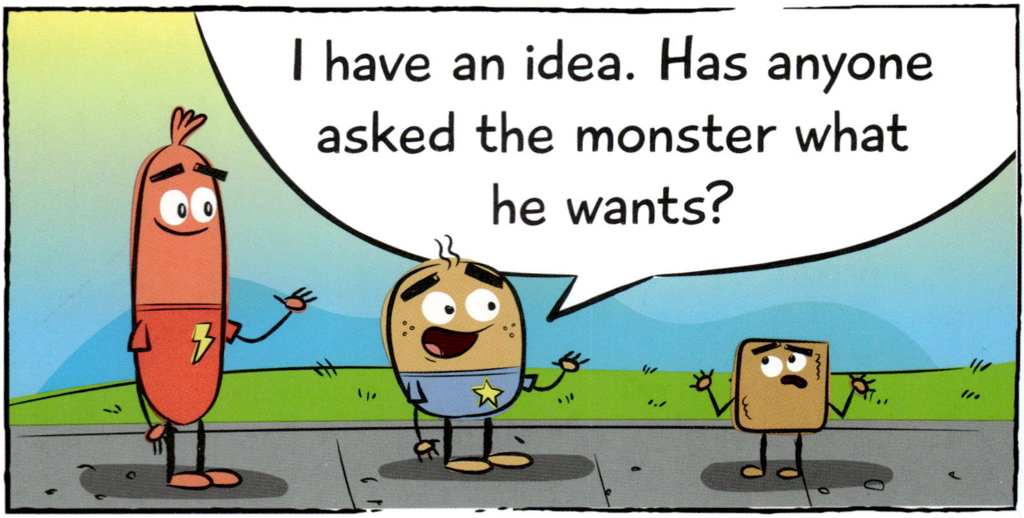
I have an idea. Has anyone asked the monster what he wants?

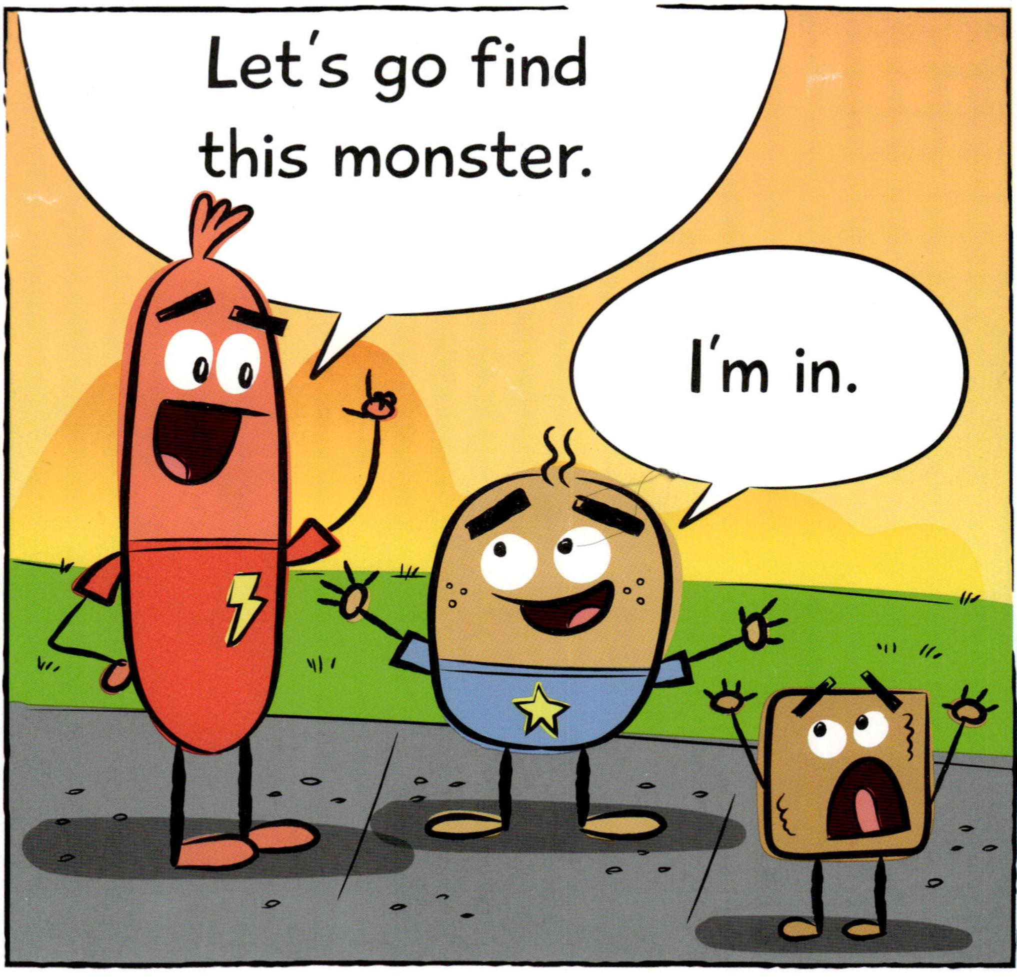
Let's go find this monster.
I'm in.

Chapter 6

MAKE A RUN FOR IT!

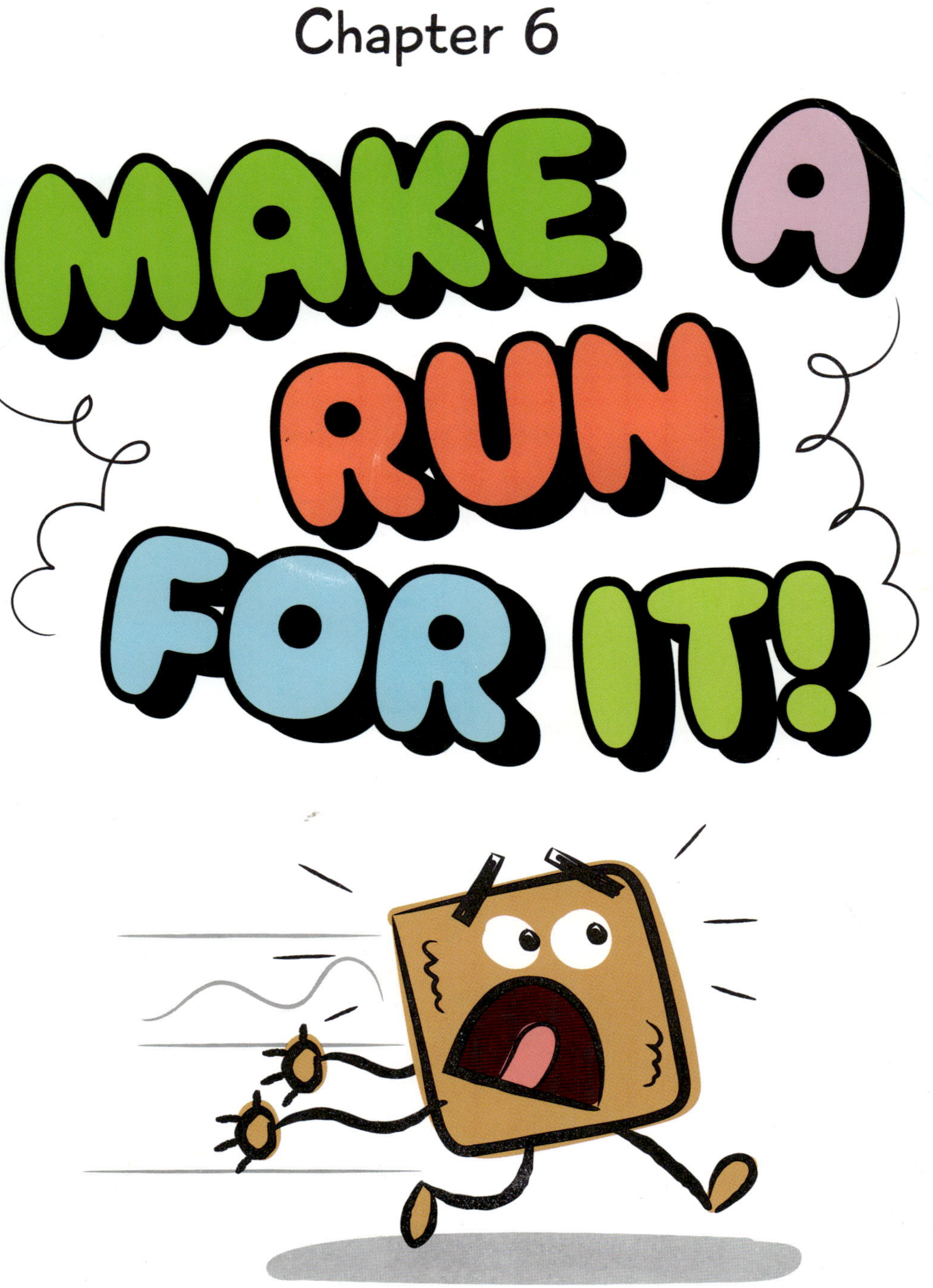

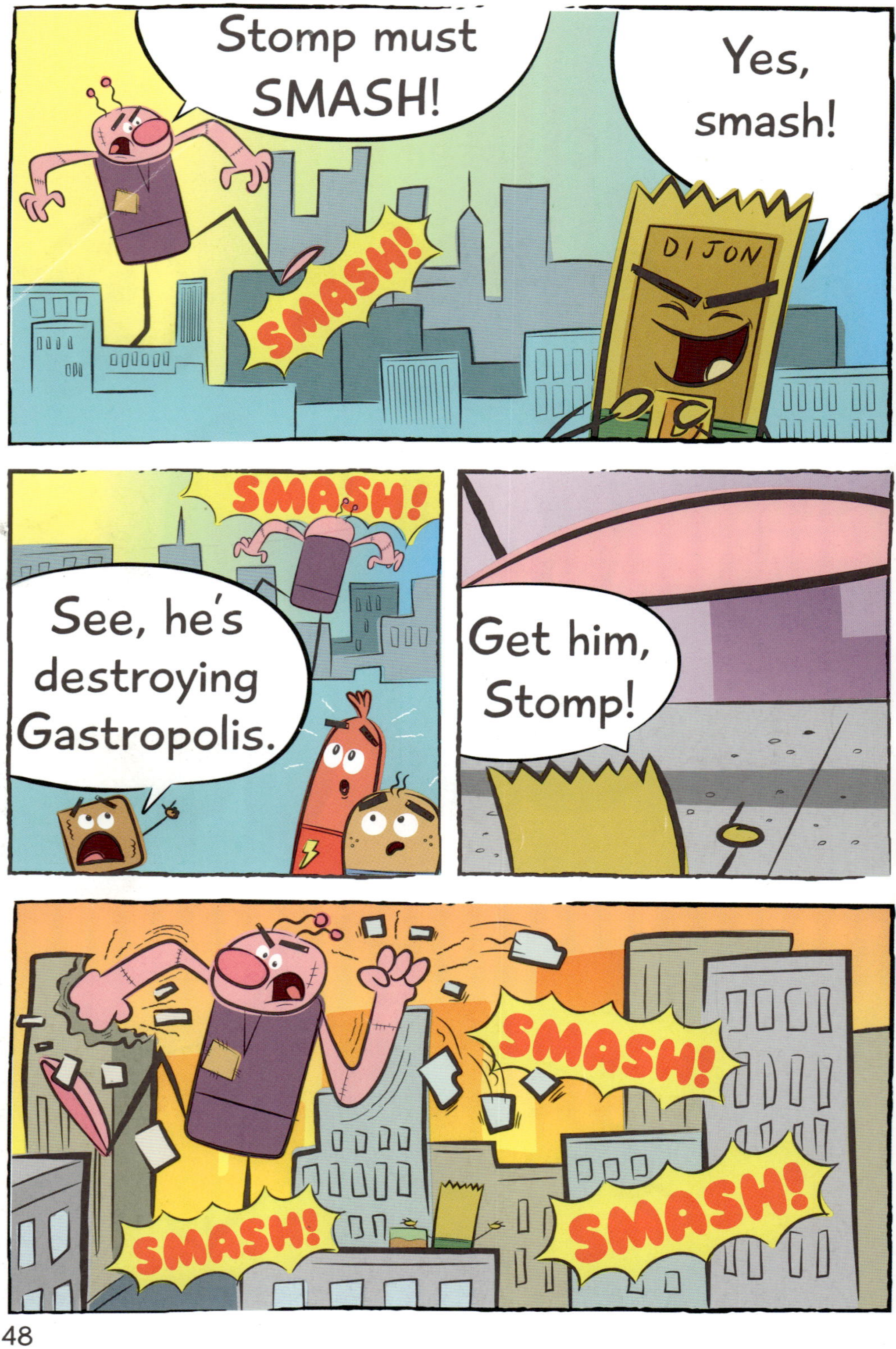
Stomp must SMASH!
Yes, smash!
SMASH!
DIJON
SMASH!
See, he's destroying Gastropolis.
Get him, Stomp!
SMASH!
SMASH!
SMASH!

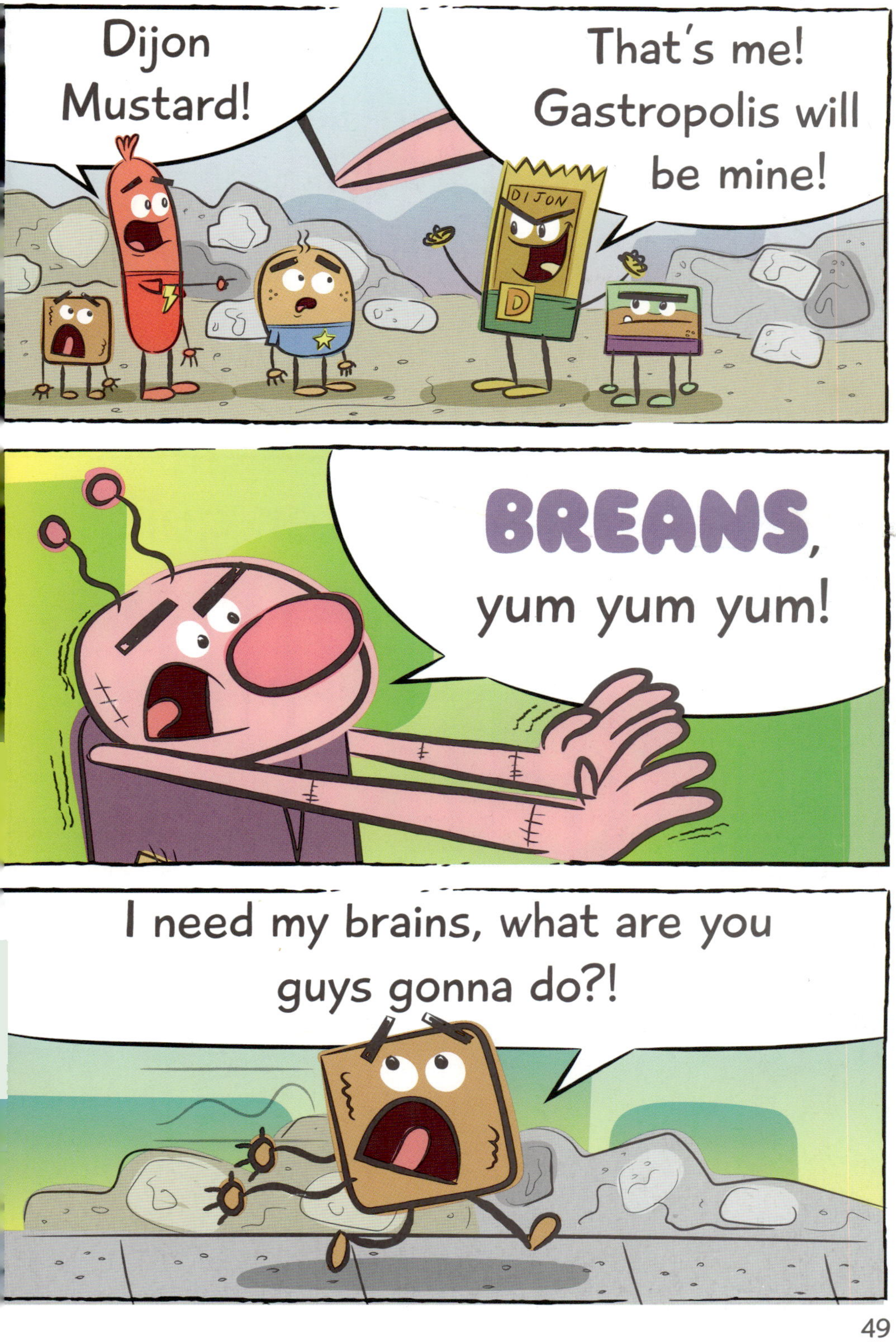
Dijon Mustard!
That's me! Gastropolis will be mine!
DIJON
D
BREANS, yum yum yum!
I need my brains, what are you guys gonna do?!

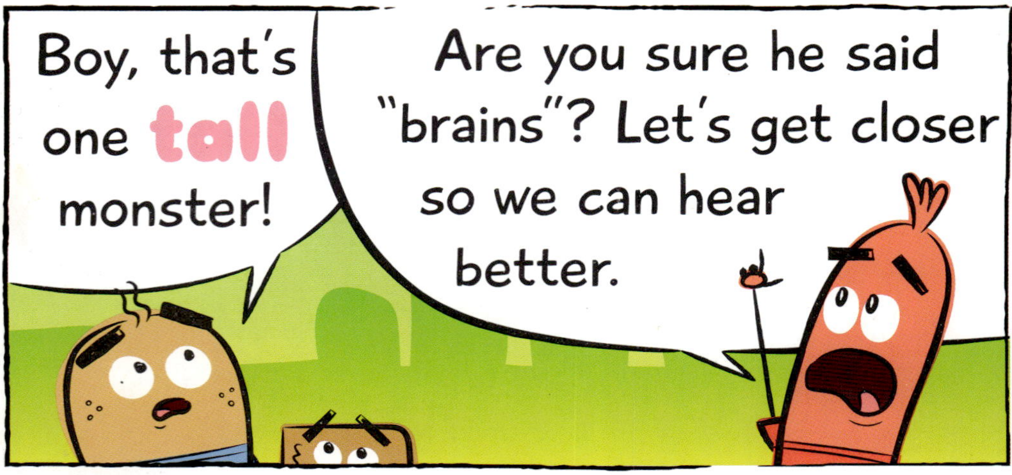
Boy, that's one tall monster!
Are you sure he said "brains"? Let's get closer so we can hear better.

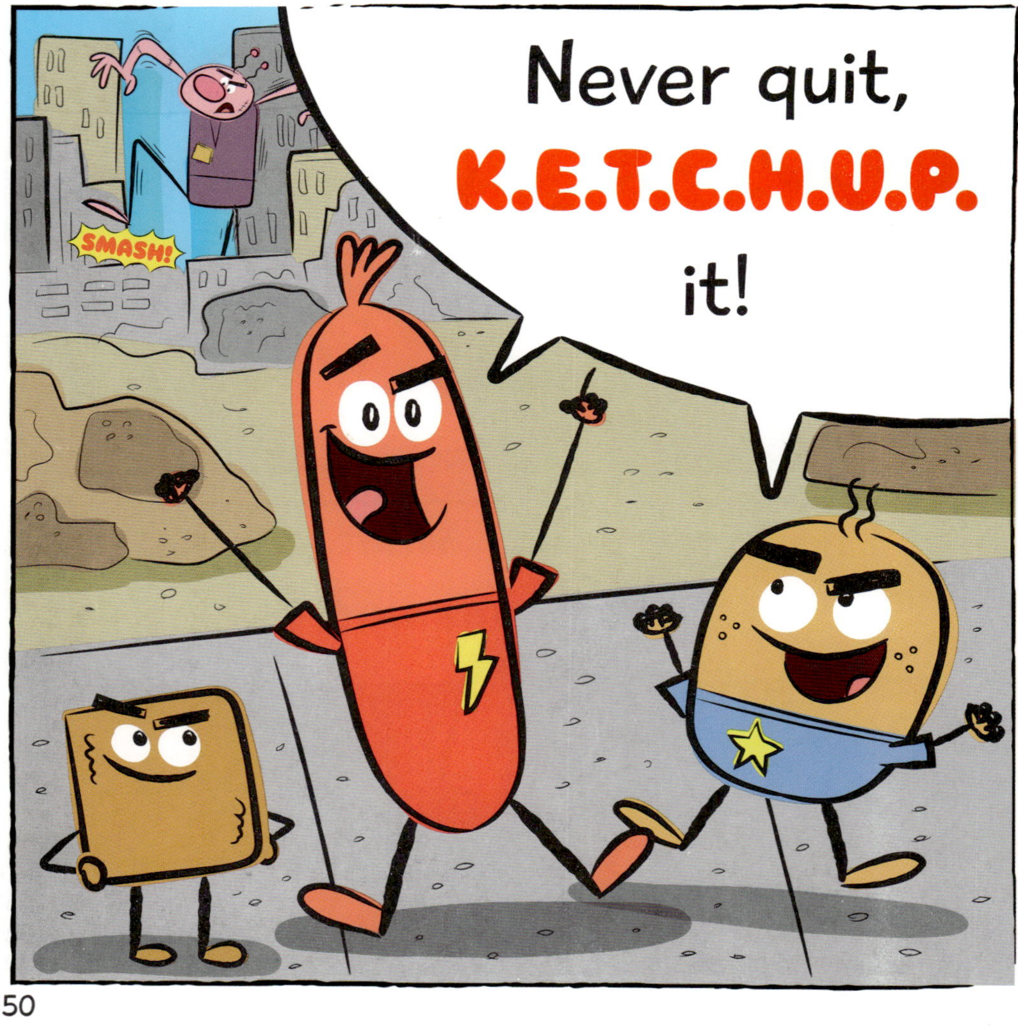
SMASH!
Never quit, K.E.T.C.H.U.P. it!

Chapter 7

LET'S TALK ABOUT IT!

Hi!

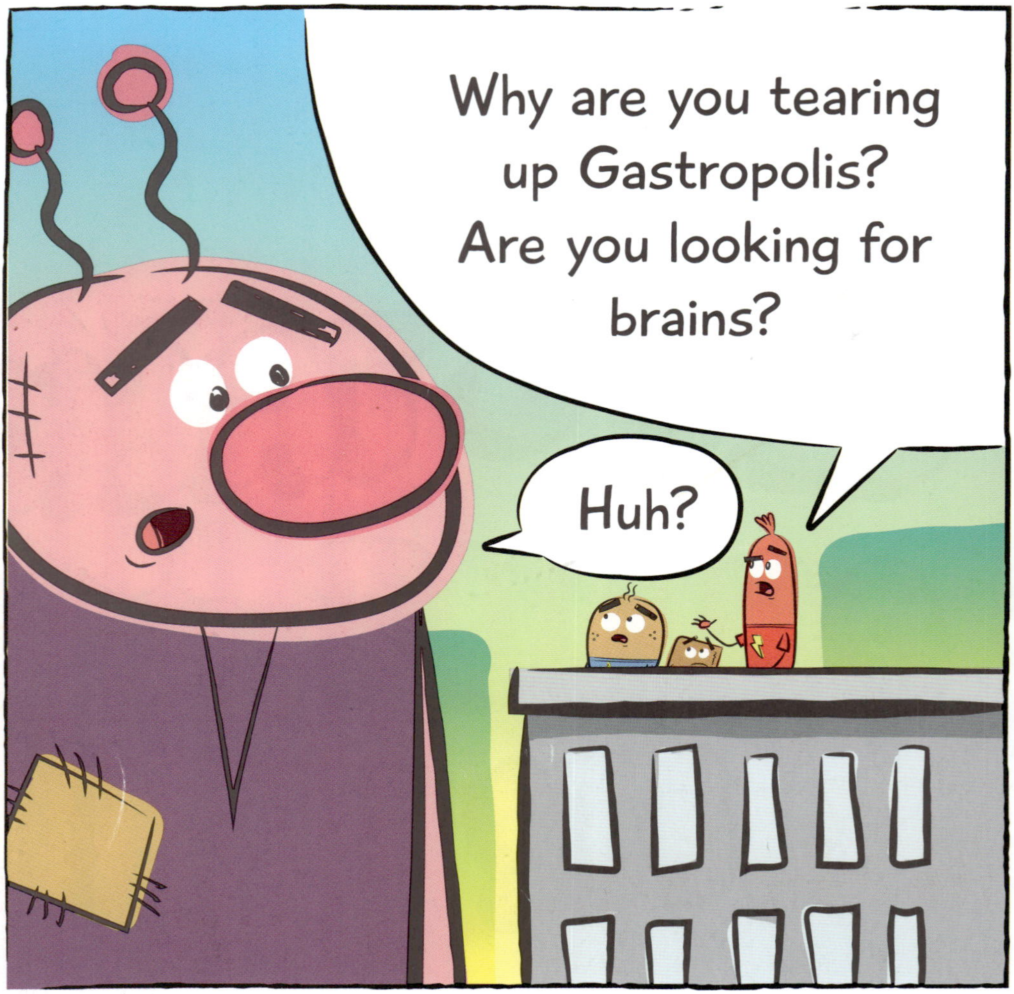
Why are you tearing up Gastropolis? Are you looking for brains?
Huh?

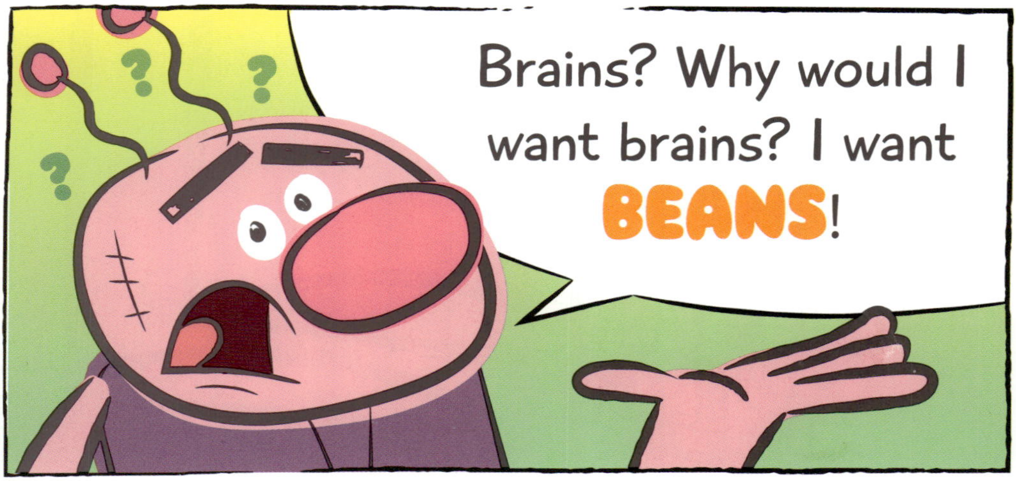
Brains? Why would I want brains? I want BEANS!

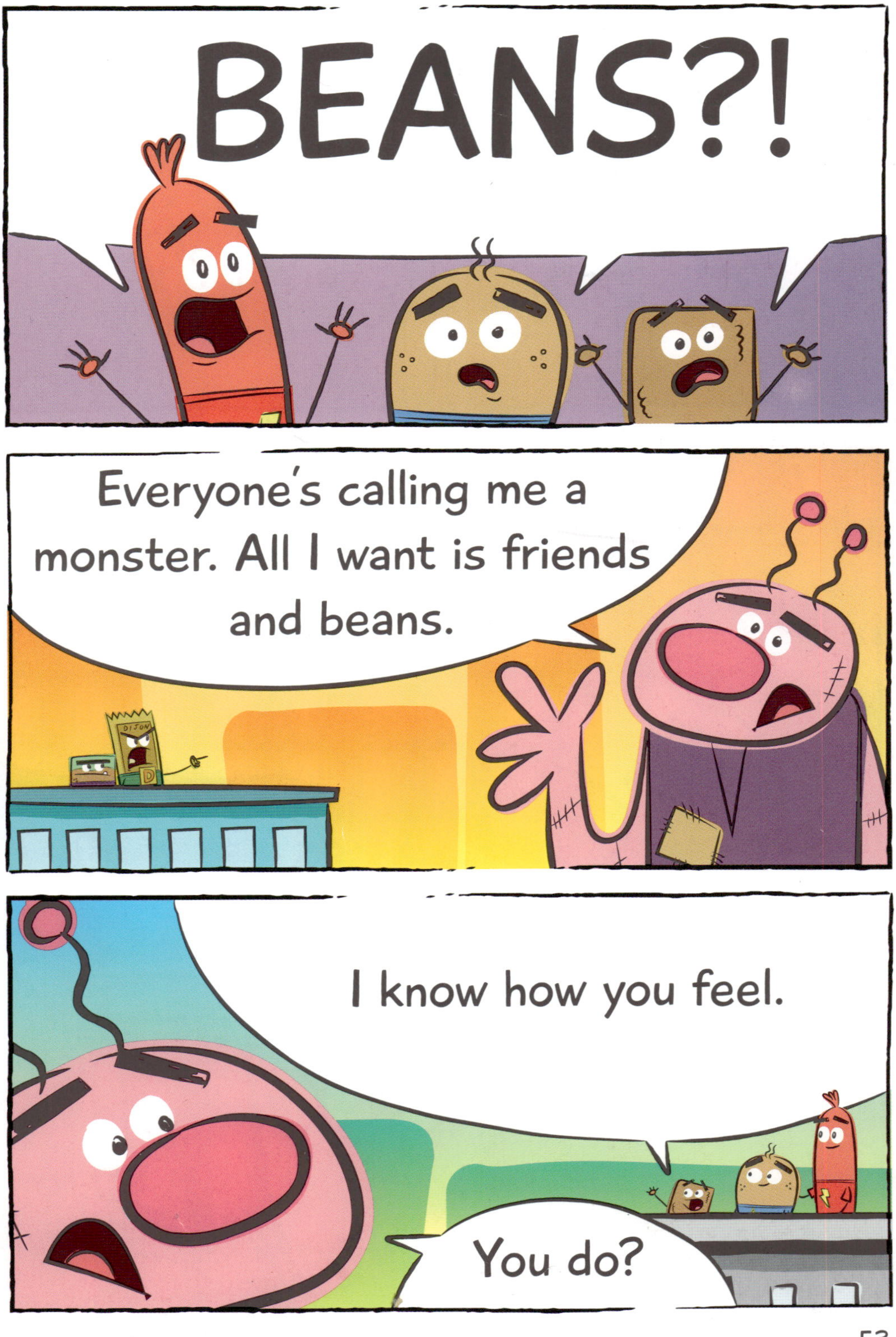
BEANS?!
Everyone's calling me a monster. All I want is friends and beans.
DIJON
D
I know how you feel.
You do?

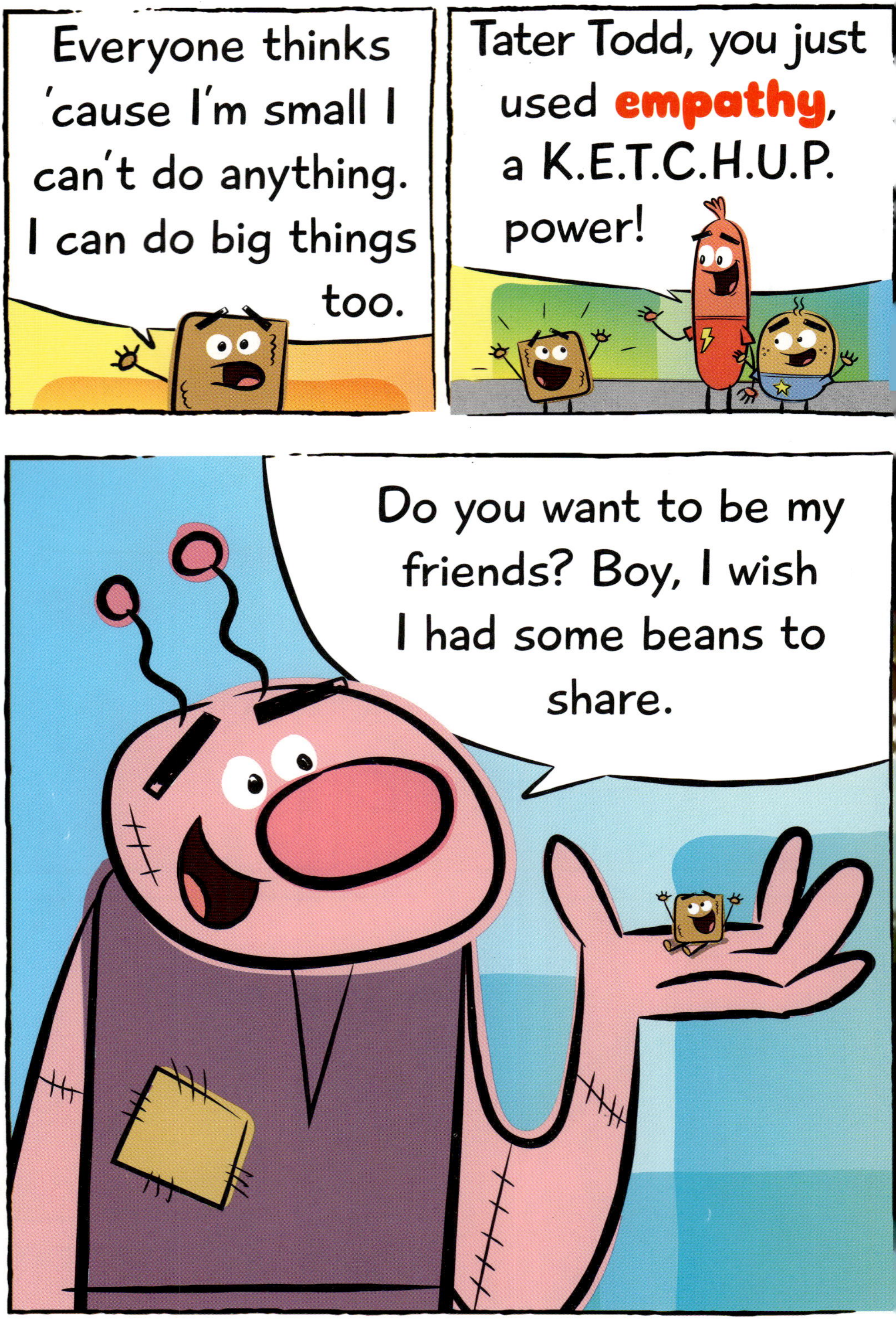
Everyone thinks 'cause I'm small I can't do anything. I can do big things too.
Tater Todd, you just used empathy, a K.E.T.C.H.U.P. power!
Do you want to be my friends? Boy, I wish I had some beans to share.

Chapter 8

BEAN BUDDIES!

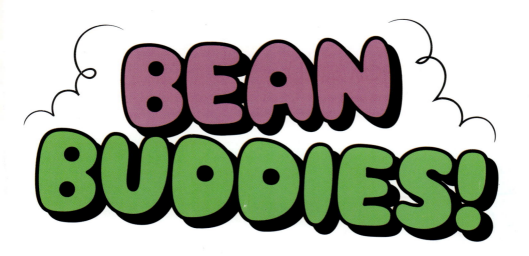

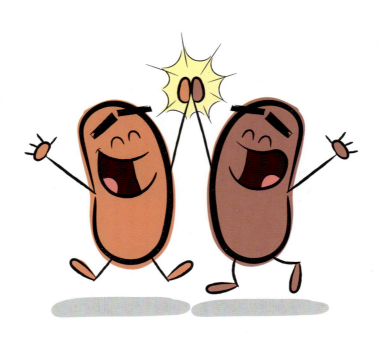

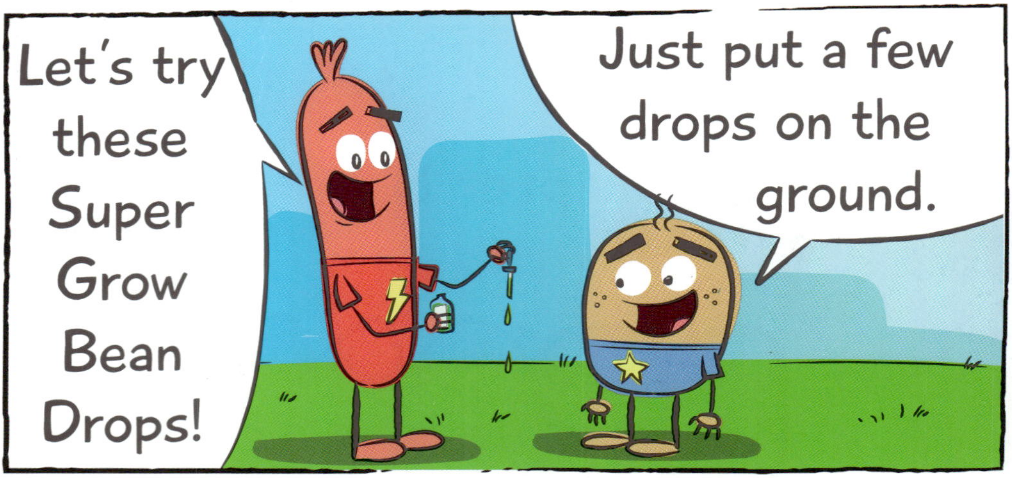
Let's try these Super Grow Bean Drops!
Just put a few drops on the ground.

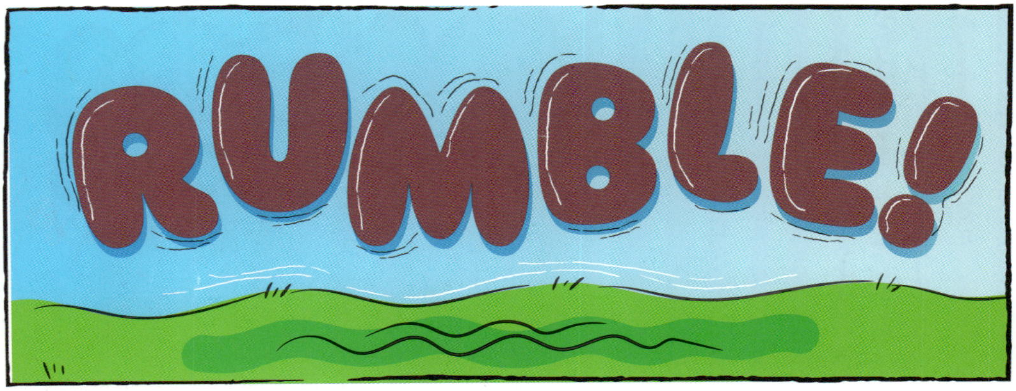
RUMBLE!

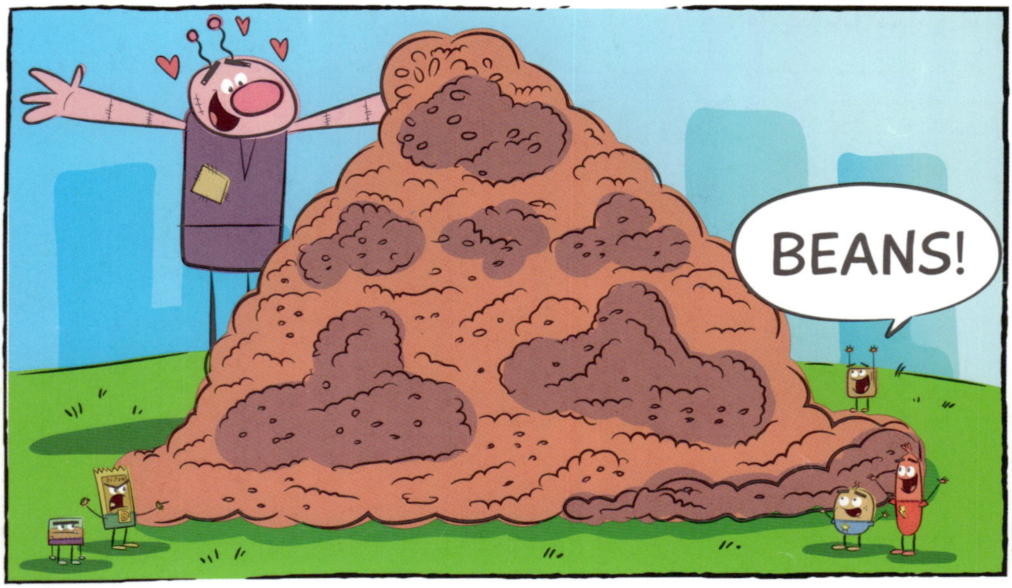
BEANS!

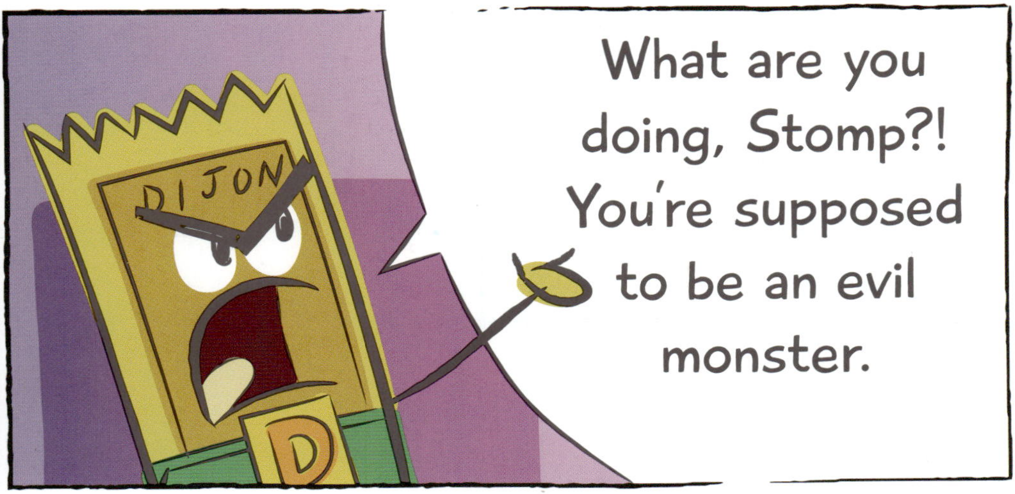
What are you doing, Stomp?! You're supposed to be an evil monster.
DIJON
D

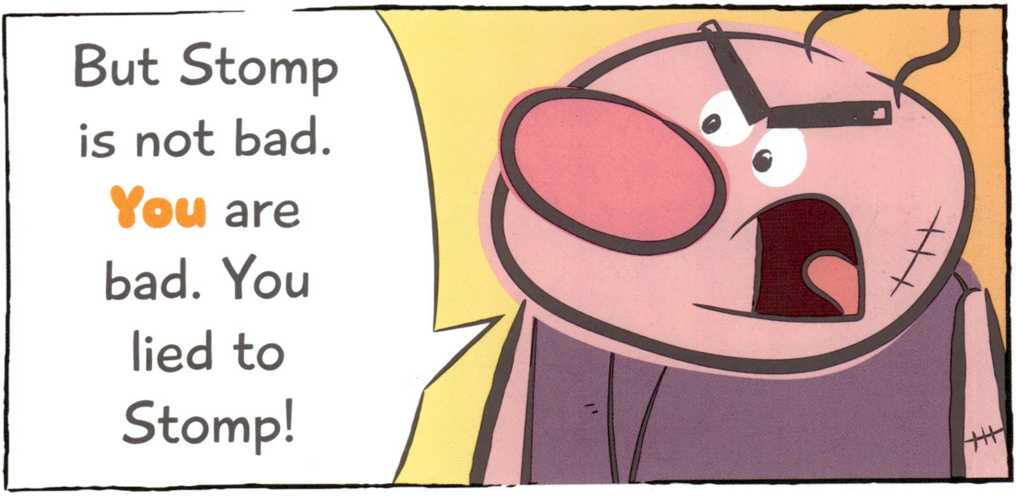
But Stomp is not bad. **You** are bad. You lied to Stomp!

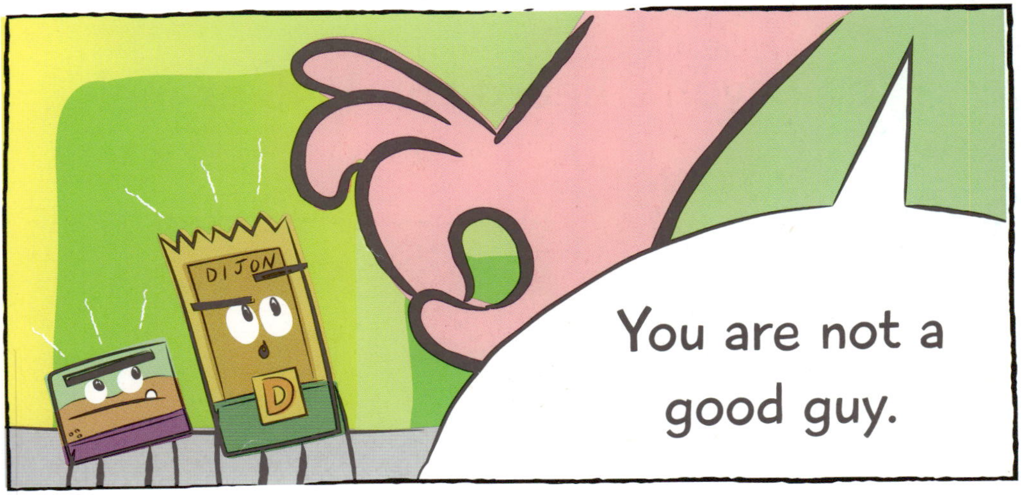
DIJON
D
You are not a good guy.

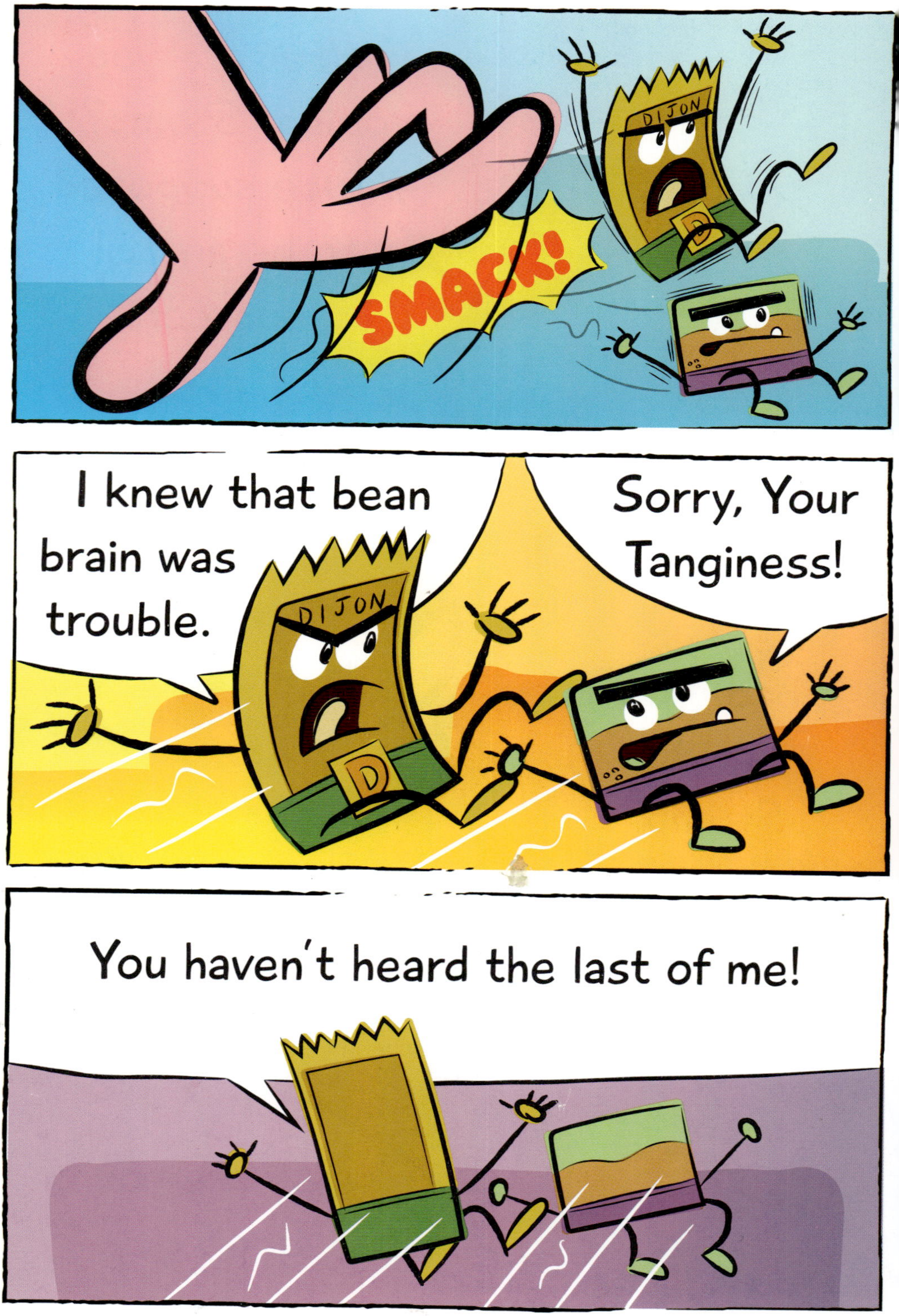
SMACK!
DIJON
D
I knew that bean brain was trouble.
Sorry, Your Tanginess!
You haven't heard the last of me!

Chapter 9

BRING ON THE YUM!

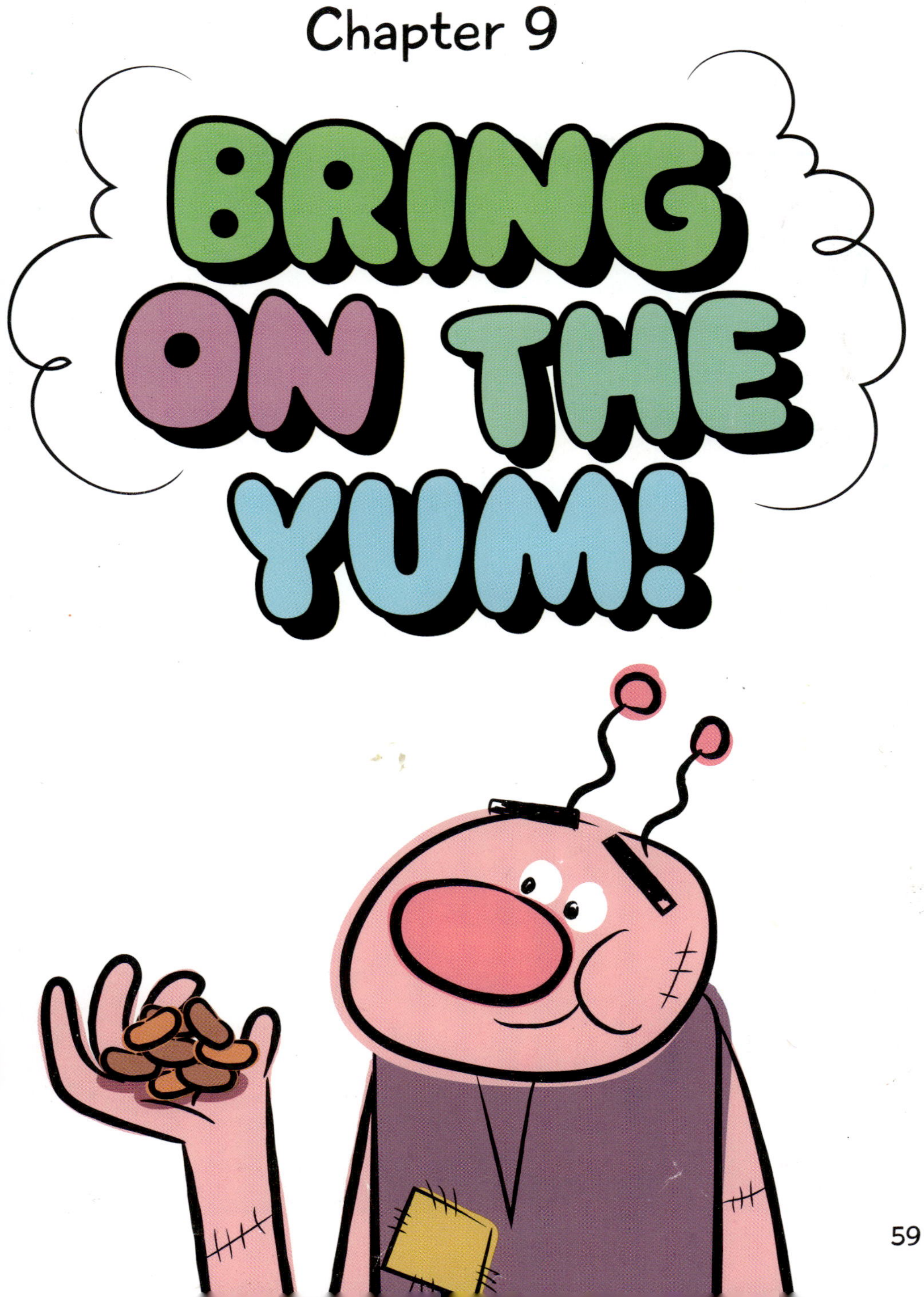

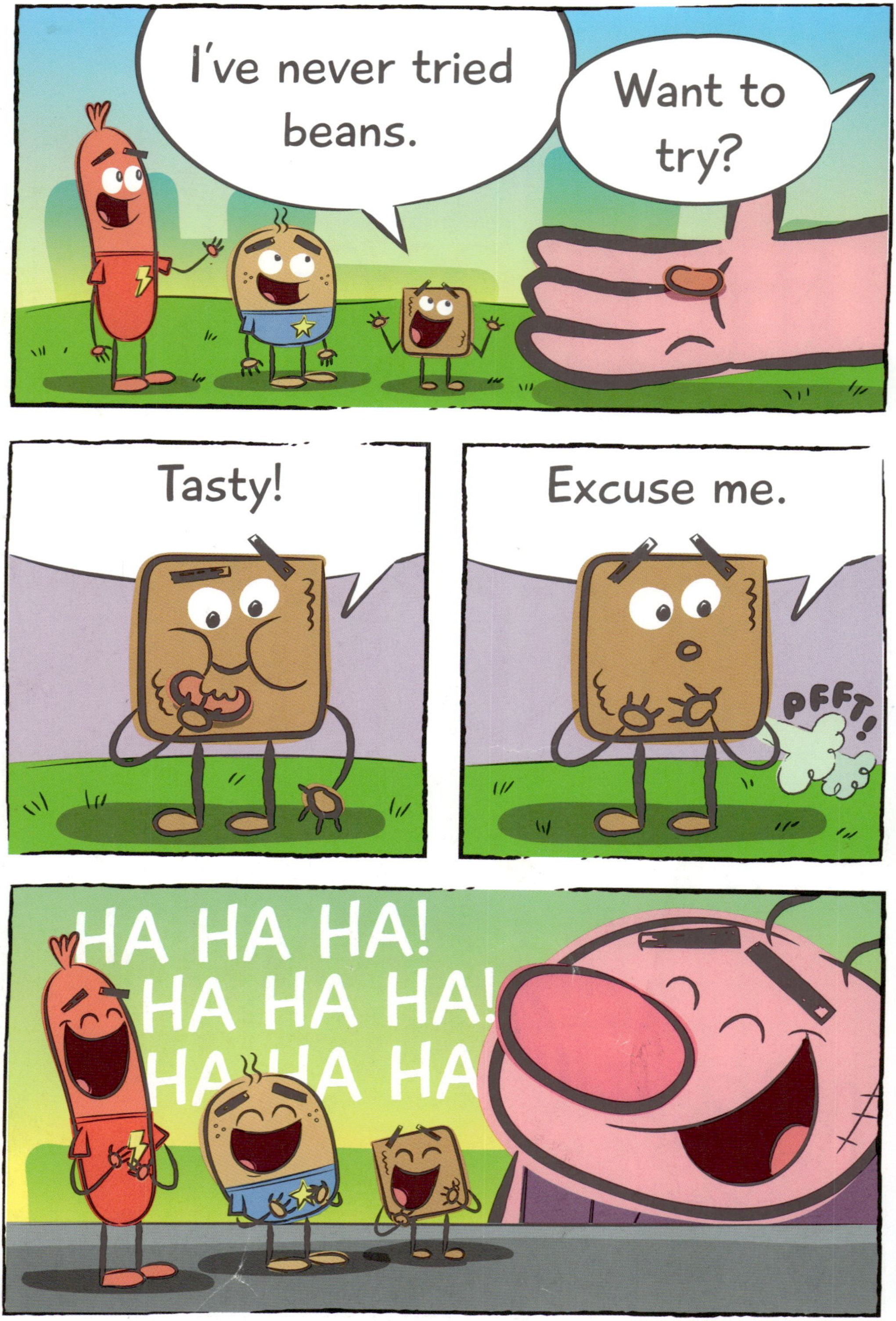
I've never tried beans.
Want to try?
Tasty!
Excuse me.
PFFT!
HA HA HA!
HA HA HA!
HA HA HA

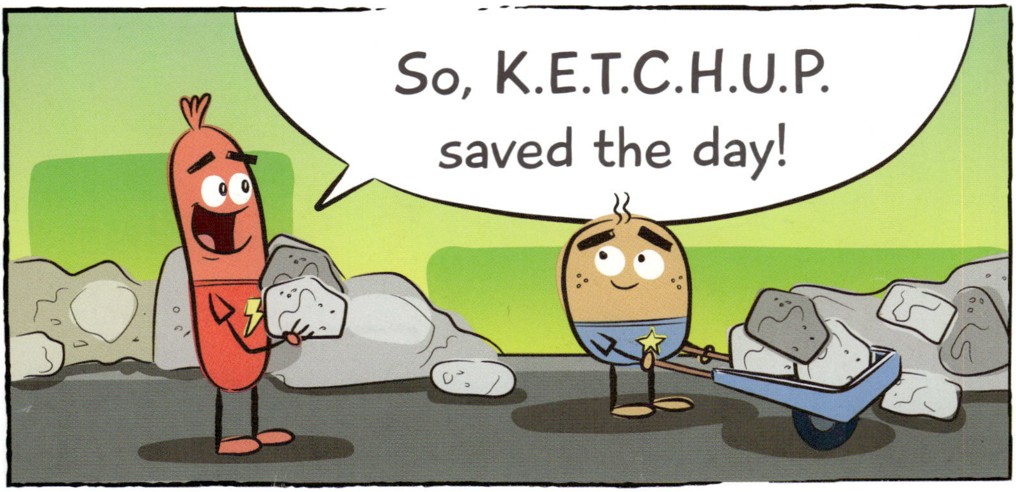
So, K.E.T.C.H.U.P. saved the day!

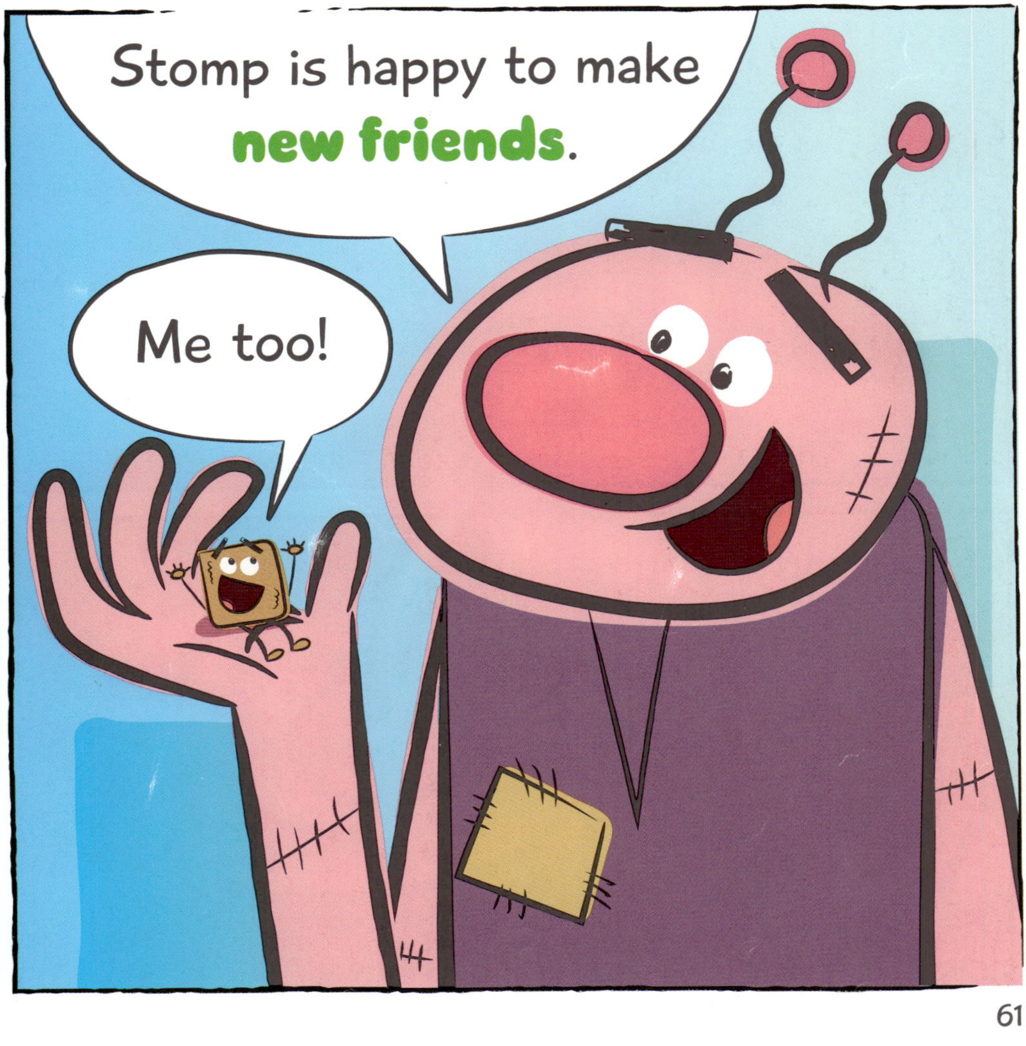
Stomp is happy to make **new friends**.
Me too!

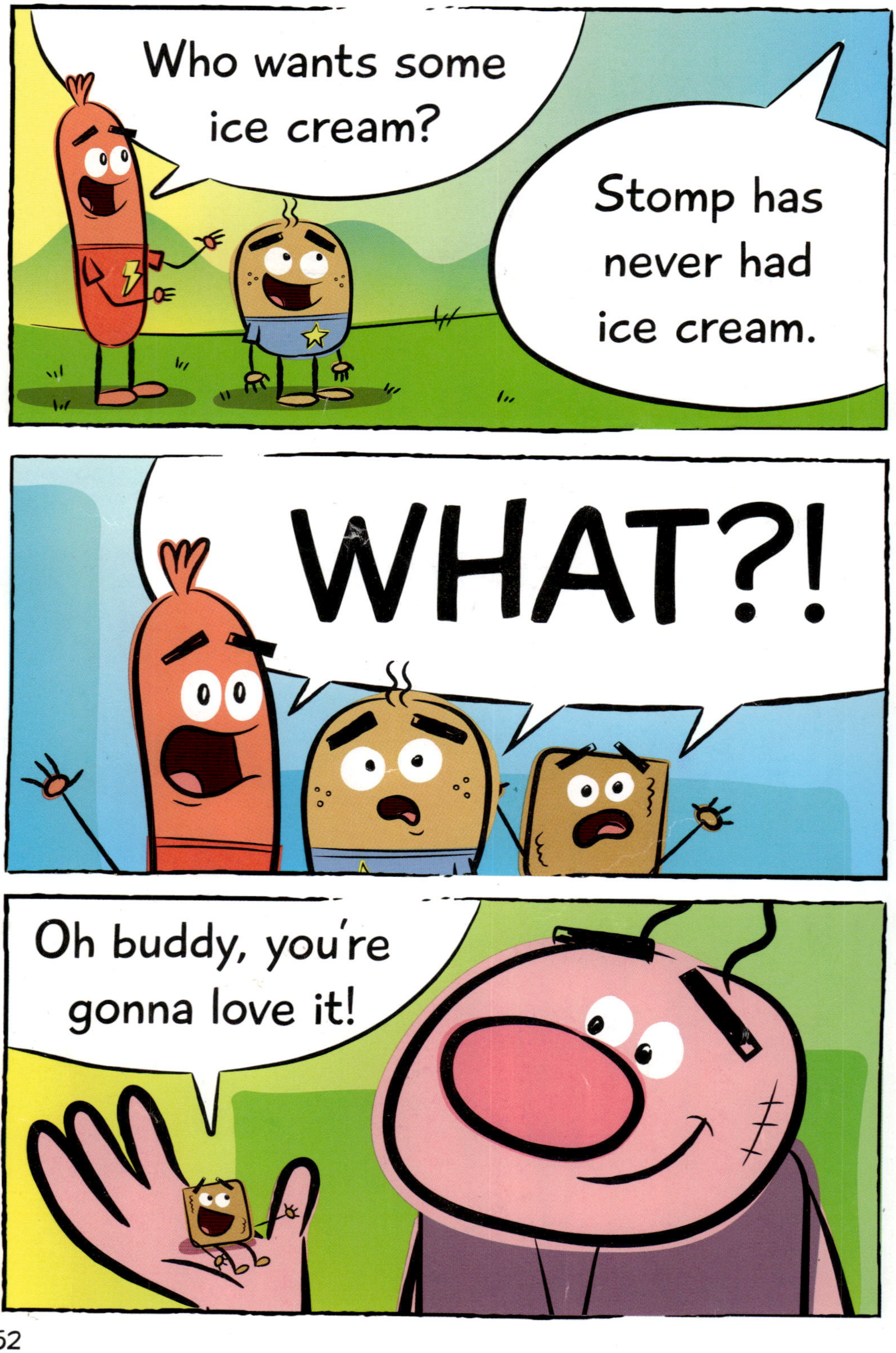
Who wants some ice cream?
Stomp has never had ice cream.
WHAT?!
Oh buddy, you're gonna love it!

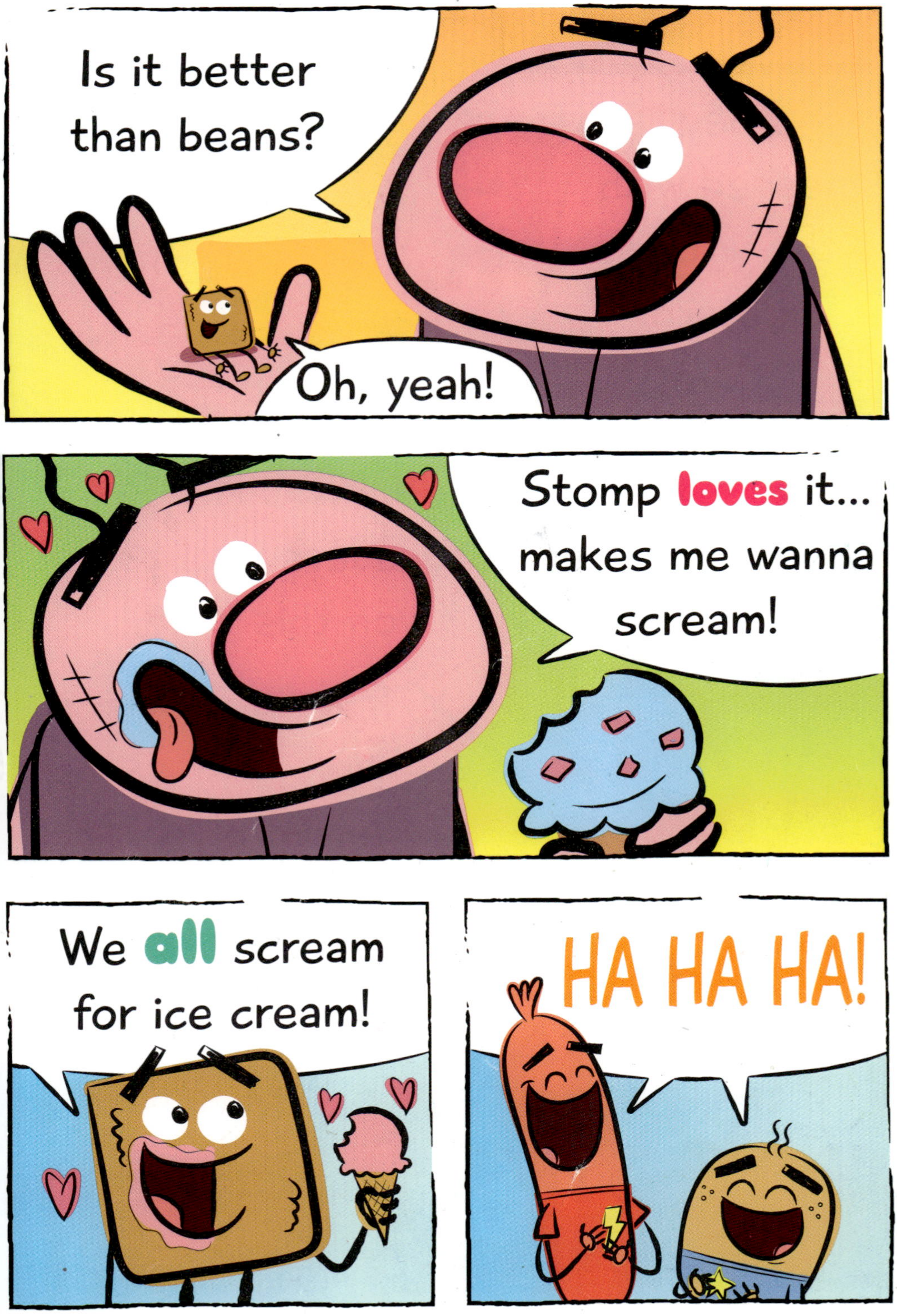

Is it better than beans?
Oh, yeah!
Stomp loves it... makes me wanna scream!
We all scream for ice cream!
HA HA HA!

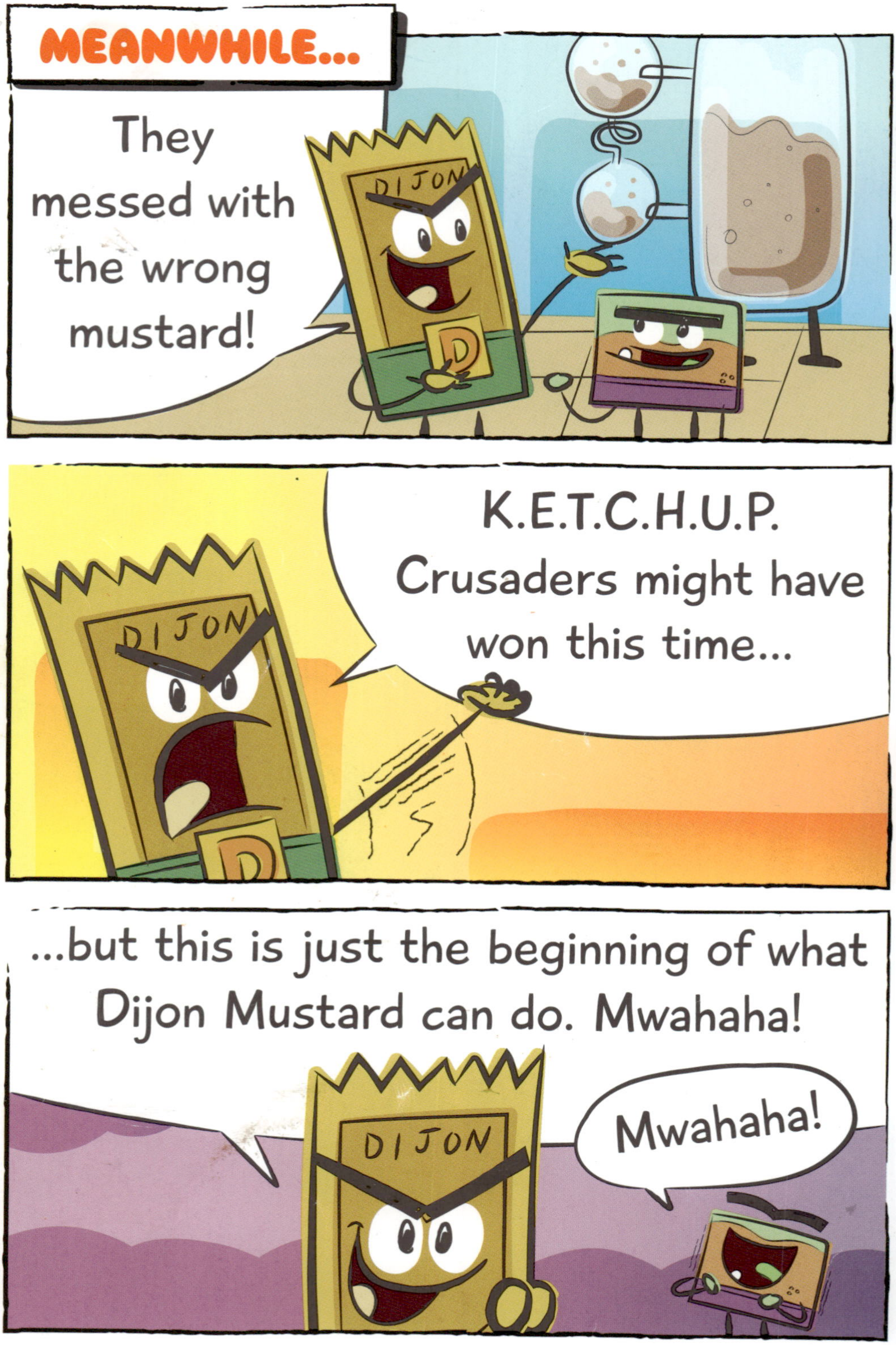
MEANWHILE...
They messed with the wrong mustard!
DIJON
D
K.E.T.C.H.U.P. Crusaders might have won this time...
DIJON
D
...but this is just the beginning of what Dijon Mustard can do. Mwahaha!
DIJON
Mwahaha!